Oh, You Wouldn't Believe It

A Novel

Written By: Morgan Klarysse Robertson

Title: Oh, You Wouldn't Believe it

ID: 1200339

Category: Romance

Copyright Year: © 2007

Language: English

Country: United States

ISBN: 978-0-6151-7380-1

WARNING!

The following novel is NOT for the light headed. If you
chose to continue beyond this page, be prepared to think
and imagine the story as it unveils before your eyes. It
even shocked me. This is not another sex story or making it
out of the hood saga, it is in a category all its own. So
sit back, grab your favorite pillow, blanket, beverage, and
whatever else you need to be comfortable and enjoy the tale.
I'll see you at the end.

Prologue

I always talked about how my day is coming. That one day my dreams would come true. In my future I would never have to worry about money or being successful.

Sometimes I look around at all that I am blessed with and just sit in awe. All I can say sometimes is "Wow this is your life girl. This is all you, you did it, you really did it".

Oh my bad, I am being so rude. Let me give you a proper introduction. My name is Clarice Taylor Harley. I am 31 years old, I work to the best of my ability, but I always manage to second guess myself.

There was a time in my life when I believed I would never be successful. I didn't have much hope at all. AT that time my name should have been Lonely Low Self-esteem Loser. At least that was the way I felt at the time. Sure my family would time that I was a pretty girl and I was smart. I knew I was smart. But there were times when I didn't feel smart enough. The most important thing to me was not being smart it was attention. Not just any kind of attention, the kind from the opposite sex. I just wanted someone to like me for me. Not because I was smart, or because I always seemed to have money in my pocket. I was good at saving. My parents had enrolled me in private school. The kids I went to school with were always taking my kindness for weakness. Not only that I got teased for being the tallest in the class, for not being light skinned, for always having my nose in a book.

The kind hearted actions only came when my mother became sick when I was 10 years old. Children can be so cruel. I only found later in life that most of the teasing was because of jealousy. Which, is why today I still say it is one thing to be envious of another but, jealousy is a sickness. You have to be sick to do some of the things I've endured. That was just elementary school.

My interest in science peeked at age 9, so did my interest in cosmetology. I was always doing my dolls hair and 'playing' in my mother's and grandmother's. Every style in a magazine or on television I tried to emulate. I loved watching how things reacted; I wanted to know how to make my own hair-relaxer. I was destined from that point on to set my career path. I was also really into skin care. I developed early so that acne thing had to be solved. I went through so many trial and error stages just to get the right medication for my skin it was ridiculous. I wanted to make something that would help my skin but would also be free of chemicals. I just wanted to avoid side effects. While I was at it I would develop the same solution for hair care. I was going to be a dermatologist and a cosmetologist; most of all successful at both professions.

Some would think it would be cool to be skipped a grade or two in school it wasn't, especially not on a social level. I was skipped to the 8th grade after being tested when I entered middle school. I should have played dumb. That is when my weight problems started coming into play. In 8th grade was when boys started noticing the changes that we as women go through during puberty. They also took a great interest in my size, particularly how much larger I was than the other girls in my class. Never mind that fact that I was taller than the other girls and I was younger as well.

I had no choice but to stay to myself. My entire class had a problem with my extra 30 pounds. Where were the guys that liked thicker girls back then? I really could have used the ego boost.

I hated being smart, I hated being over weight. What 11 year old do you know is a on a diet? I was stuck if I stayed the same size I get teased if I went on a diet some one would find a problem with that. I cried every day for at least an hour, then did my homework, read a book, ate dinner, got in the tub, and off to bed. I didn't sleep most nights because I dreaded going to school. I used to love going to school. That feeling changed so quickly.

High school was no better. The teasing got worse. The worse, and more crude the comment the more I sought comfort in food. I know I shouldn't have done that, but nobody was stopping me either. By the time I was in my 20's I didn't know I was pretty and I put up with pretty much anything to avoid being lonely. I wish I would have realized that I was better than that, because how I conduct my life now is all about my past.

The one guy in all that time that even paid attention to me was a 'hook up'. Some friend of mines throw away guy. Ladies if you don't want him don't give that mess to your friend let the next woman find him some where. I have never accepted a hook up since. I was 16 years old still a virgin and in college. As soon as the men at school found out I was not 18 they backed off. Except for him, but he only paid attention long enough to get me pregnant. Jonathon promised my marriage and the practically the world if I would have his baby. Then he woke up around the time I was six months along with my daughter and realized that children cost money. Money he didn't want to spend. There went my life. I felt had no choice but to get a job to care for my baby and me.

Thankfully I had two parents that wanted to see me succeed. They told me that they would support me and I didn't have to work. I am so grateful for that. So I dropped down to part time in college. I still felt I needed to do for me and my child. I enrolled in beauty school during the day and took classes online. I took a job at a restaurant waiting on tables, which is where I met Harrison. We've been friends ever since.

Once I finished beauty school I enrolled full time in school again. It only took a year for me to get my license and I was still enrolled in college so I was still on track for graduating on time. Three years later I was on my way to medical school to become a dermatologist. I was in a program that allowed me at the end of 5 years to have my master's in Chemistry as well. I told you I wanted to make

the products I recommend. My master's and my cosmetologist
license help with paying for some of medical school.

The hardest part was being away from Amaris. But I was
doing all this for her and me too but mostly her. She
needed me. Jonathon, well I took him to child support.
Would you believe he had the nerve to ask for a DNA test.
He got it and he had egg on his face. Hello you took my
virginity, moving on.

Introductions

    My establishment Naturally Creative Salon and Barber Shop has three locations. The cornerstone location Baltimore, Maryland, Philadelphia, Pennsylvania, and where I currently reside Atlanta, Georgia. The shop is located on Peachtree Street; I don't think I could have selected a better location. Yes of course location seems to be everything these days but if you have an excellent clientele base with reputation to accompany it you could be working out of a row house turned salon and still bring in the dollars. Which is, by the way is how I got started in Baltimore.

    I always arrived at the shop at 7:30 a.m. sharp. We open at 9:30 a.m.; I require that all stylist, barbers and technicians arrive at 8:45 a.m. It was a practice that was started in the first location in Baltimore. Why do I arrive so early? Simple when I started this business I made God a promise that I would always acknowledge him first. Everyone that knows me will tell you that I've been through some things, but I endured it all because my life has a purpose. I believe that everyone should recognize the power that maintains our very existence in Him. I ain't preaching just giving credit where it is due.

Now I'm not the only one up this early. I am certainly not the only one God made a night owl that has to deal with business hours. There is my Ace, my business partner and my best friend. The person that has been through everything with me before we even had a business plan. That one person who other than my parents, that I feel I can trust on a financial level. Harrison Lamont Caleb Brown, 30 years old, there is no point in asking why his parents couldn't make up their minds and pick one middle name. As an inside thing I call him "L.C.", double meaning you might just find that out later.

As I said before I am **NOT** a morning person so you better believe if I don't have any appointments between the hours of 11:30a.m. To 1:00p.m. I am out for the count in my cozy office. I rarely take advantage of that luxury. I love my office I had every piece hand selected, every piece is

unique to my persona and check this out right I did it on
an average budget. I really didn't need to but I believe in
investing my money on more profitable things.

"L.C." and I decided when we first started out that
our days should begin with prayer and end with prayer. We
all need it regardless of how close we think we are to God.
Someone is always out there trying to throw salt in your
game. Not everyone is happy to see you succeed.

***

With a classic name like mine you would think my
husband's name is the same way. Not even close, but if you
know anything about the bible; then you know his name is
not something his parents just made up. My husband age 35
Adonai David Lavi Harley, but family and friends call him
"Nai". In the business world he is David, you know how
people can butcher a name. And yes seems like his parents
had the same problem Harrison's did. I love my baby just
the same.

Then there is my daughter, if she isn't the mirror
image of me then I don't know what is. I surely spit that
girl out. Amaris Liana Harley is 15 years old she is far

from your hot in the pants out of control teenage girl. I made a point to be as open as possible with her so that she will not repeat history. She absorbs everything I do and holds on to it.

Oh yeah more about my hubby. Let me tell you, it would not matter what shade Nai came in he would still be gorgeous, not just fine. Don't get me wrong he isn't a pretty boy; he just takes good care of himself. Nai has the most hypnotizing gray eyes with a hint of brown, although he always tells me he loves my maple brown eyes better. His deep, smooth, soft voice that comes from those full pillows he calls his lips. My man is border line brown skin depending on the day he looks like yellow, other times he looks caramel. Nai is a CPA, certified public account, with his own accounting and investment firm. He started it right after he acquired his master's degree and….

"Baby, are you awake?" Nai says softly.

Umm, that man just whispered in my ear got to go.

"Hey baby, good morning. Did you sleep well?" I said softly after turning myself to face Nai.

"It will be a better morning once you give me those lips." Nai kissed me softly. "Girl, you taste better every time I kiss you, I Love You Forever." That is what Nai has said to me every day starting six months after we met, which was April 7, 2000. We said 'I do' on October 7, 2000 6:45pm that evening. I had peeked at his watch while our bishop pronounced us Mr. & Mrs. Adonai David Lavi Harley. He said the whole name too. Our anniversary was less than a week away and Nai had a big surprise for me and he wasn't giving up any clues either. This was going to be our 5th Wedding Anniversary.

"I love you forever my husband." I responded as Nai went to work on my collar bone. There was a time where I doubted ever being able to say the words my husband. About three or four months prior to meeting Nai I had taken the advice of a man I just couldn't seem to have. I had turned my feelings for men I dated off completely. If they did get the privilege of sleeping with me which happened once; they were the ones really feeling me and not the other way around. It was unnatural for me to be this way but because I got hurt too many times it was just best for me to get what I could out of the date and ball.

My collar bone is my hot spot, it drove me almost mad, and Nai knew it. Nai had the body of a Greek god, no joke he was black Zeus. He had no chest hair on his chiseled torso; his pecks are just the right size not too bulky. If you needed to study the muscles on the human body he would be the perfect model. He has abs that would put a washboard to shame. And his legs, he definitely held on to that football physique. Now, unlike a good deal of men his hands and feet are well taken care of and the whole body is soft.

"Nai, baby…honey…oh Nai slow down."

"For what, stop playing I know what I'm doing," He said as he moved further south towards my breasts, paying very close attention to every inch. "…I let you slide the past two nights because you were working late in the shop."

"I know but it seems like you are trying to make me climax already."

"You know that is torture for me to lay there next to my wife and not touch her." He stated in between kisses to my neck and ear lobe. "All those curves on that soft body, you have got to be kidding me."

"Yes baby, I'm sorry I know how much you missed me I don't know why you put up with me." As I stroked his manhood to signal him to continue; "I promise I'll make it all worth it on our anniversary. Now show me exactly how much you missed me." I wrapped my arms around Nai.

"You know why I put up with you, because you are my rare diamond. I can't help but to hold on to you." Nai said.

We fell into a passionate kiss just as if we were newly weds again. Nai was always gentle with me, in all of our interactions. The way he touched me with such care was always spine tingling. Even the simplest action as holding my hand Nai was gentle; I could always take comfort in the fact that I was safe with him.

***

"Did I satisfy you baby? Nai said as he washed her back. Nai always takes care of me he practically tries to make sure I never have to lift a finger.

"I don't think I will ever be dissatisfied with anything you do for, with or to me. You always ask me that, my answer is never going to change."

"I just had to make sure; I never know when I might slip. You know I can't live without you." Nai said as he began to give attention to my sacred center.

"I can do that myself, I know how you are," as I was grabbing the cloth away from him; "you are not going to make us late for church."

"Come on baby, we won't be late. Besides we are married, it's not like we have to lie on the altar and repent our lustful sins."

"Now you know you are wrong for that, I am getting out of this tub now so we all can have breakfast. It would not

be good for someone's stomach to be talking during the
sermon. Or did you forget about Amaris?"

"Come to think of it I could use one of your
'anointed' Sunday morning breakfast masterpieces. No I did
not forget about my baby girl, who could forget someone as
beautiful and smart as her mother?"

"Does that mean you want pancakes, an omelet, bacon,
sausage and a big glass of milk this morning?" Clarice said
as I finished putting on my undergarments; slipping back
into my robe, walking downstairs to the second floor and to
Amaris' room.

"Amaris, are you up yet? I'm going down stairs to
make breakfast. Do you want anything special?"

Amaris opened the door. Here stood the spitting image
of me, height, shape, complexion, eye color, dimples and
all. I love my daughter like no other mother could. We grew
up together; best friends forever bonded.

"Hey Mommy I was just picking out what I wanted to
wear. Whatever you fix is fine with me, but can I just have
egg whites today?" Her voice even sounded like mine.

"Sure whatever you like."

"Hey Mommy I'm almost done can I help you cook?"

"You know I don't mind, it will more likely get your
daddy down here faster." We both laughed, -- Sunday morning.

***

"God you knew what you were doing when you made
Clarice. If I haven't thanked you lately, I am certainly
doing it now. I love my wife. Man, all those men that
cheated, dogged, ignored, or just plain used her; I
appreciate their lack of common sense. I just couldn't
imagine with her not as my wife." Nai finished making sure
his face and hair was on point. There is not a thing wrong
with a man that takes care of his appearance, it's a
wonderful thing. As he was finishing, the aroma of
breakfast had moved its way up through the house and to his
nose.

"Time to eat, I can taste it already." It seemed as if
it took no time for Nai to make it to the kitchen from the
third floor. Now of course with his six foot five inch
frame why would not be able to take two flights of stairs
by leaps and bounds.

"Baby, that smells so good." Nai sits down at the
kitchen table. "Can we bless the food now?"

"Thank you, baby but I can't take all the credit. Our
daughter helped me." I smiled as I pointed out that little
fact to Nai.

"Well baby girl if you keep helping your mother like this you are sure to make some good man very happy one day." He stood up and gave Amaris a hug and a kiss.

"Thanks, Daddy but I still have a lot of practice to get in. I only cooked the eggs." Amaris was very humble. We all sat down at the table. Nai blessed the food as always and we had breakfast. As a usual part of our Sunday morning routine, Nai washed the dishes so that we could finish getting dressed and put the finishing touches on our makeup and hair. Amaris had learned a great deal about hair care and makeup from me and she knew how to utilize those skills. My baby girl was all grown up, well almost, and fabulous. An half an hour had past and we were heading out the door. Which car we rode in depended on mostly which one was closest to the end of the drive way. This Sunday we rode in Nai's new Jeep.

***

That's the way life goes

The majority of the time Nai would take Amaris to school. I would always have at least two early appointments at the shop. Besides that was my time to meditate. Maybe it was the fact that our anniversary was less than a week away. Nai was like a mad man, like a man who had done without the feeling of being inside a woman's, more importantly this woman's sweet center. Nai always made sure that I never doubted his love for me. He always did something special, something different everyday just to reassure me of his undying love and his passion and commitment to our marriage.

There was a time when I thought me and marriage, a husband, happiness would never happen. I just knew I would be destined to be alone until the day I died.

To me Nai was the perfect husband. He always kept an even tone even when I was hyped up to argue. That wasn't often and my little temper did show itself after a short while. Nai helped me so much when we first met. By the time he proposed, all my inhibitions were gone, all my doubts, baggage you name it were gone. I couldn't help but to say yes through all my tears…I had my dream proposal as well. Ever since I can remember my mother telling my how by the time she and my father were together six months he wanted, my daddy made it official that he wanted my mommy to be his wife. I always dreamed of love like that and now I have it. What more could I ask for?

If I worked late at the shop he would bring dinner and we would eat in my office. When Amaris worked with me on the weekend, Nai would bring us all dinner and would take Amaris home. He would sit up until I came home and walked into his arms.

***

I love being in his embrace— off went that alert on my phone. I know who it is.

"Harrison, I'm in the house and a little preoccupied." I said as I pressed the talk button on the phone.

"Come on Lady you know it won't be long." He always called me that.

"Can we discuss whatever it is tomorrow?"

L.C. is always very determined and of course makes a point to talk about whatever is on his mind especially when he has his thoughts together.

"Real quick man, come on just listen."

"Alright L.C. what is it? If it's not as urgent as you are making it, I'm driving to your house and I'm going to pluck you real good." We laughed.

Nai was hitting my spot and I was trying my best not to let L.C. hear. Nai was never threatened by the fact that my best friend was a man. It seemed to arouse him even more when he knew that I was tortured in my own way when he caressed my body.

"Check this out right, some money people called me up yesterday wanting to invest in us opening up a distribution office that sold exclusively our products. That is your creative genius at work. They want open four locations." Now "L.C." was getting to the good part.

"Okay I'll retract my previous statement."

"Good here are the market locations they are going for; Atlanta, Baltimore, Philadelphia, and New York."

"Cool, so when are they sending the figures? You know giving us an official proposal, talk is cheap. I'm not going to hold that thought for too long without something in writing. Plus, you know I got to run that past David to make sure everything is cool on the accounting end."

"David, what, I thought you always ran things by Nai, he is our accountant, and the best." I laughed so hard I almost dropped the phone.

"Oh damn, man okay you got me, duh Nai David, the same person." I was still laughing

"Yeah that's what you get. I told you that it could wait until tomorrow. See now you confused yourself, go to bed Harrison."

"Yeah I'm going."

"Can I go back to my evening with my husband? I so can not wait until you get married, but even then you still are going bug me to death. I still got love for you though."

"Alright I'll say good night to you both. Because I know Nai was sitting there the whole time. Oh, tell my god daughter to call me."

"Bye Harrison."

By now I was smiling hard at Nai. "You play too much." I whispered as I put my arms around Nai's neck and kissed him gently.

"I couldn't help it. You are just so desirable, I couldn't resist." He started going back after that spot, driving me to ecstasy. Nai stopped for a moment. "Do you have any early morning appointments tomorrow?"

"Actually I don't, I had only planned to take care of some ordering during the early part of the day, maybe take a walk-in or two."

Nai looked perplexed. "Well, how about you call me here when you are done with all that."

"Oh, you are not going in the office in the morning?"

"I do have that option you know. Besides whatever important deadlines I have to meet can be taken care of from here. They would be last minute anyway. You know I can't stand having things just sitting around. But that is also why I have employees."

"Okay mister business man, I hear you talking, well what I have to take care of has to be done in the office. My list is there as well. I think since I got to go you should go."

Nai let out a light chuckle. "Last time I checked you owned a business too, at least that's how I remember meeting you. Maybe I'm mistaken."

I smiled. "No you are certainly not mistaken, I remember that day just like it was yesterday. We had only been open six months." I smiled as I reminisced over the events of that day.

***

Nai had come into the shop at 9:30 a.m. He was wearing a full beard that day, a tan button down shirt, olive green khaki pants, a pair of butterscotch timberland boots, a single sterling silver chain, and a single diamond stud in his left ear. Nai wasn't wearing any particular brand of cologne but he smelled so good. Nai had locks at about medium length they were maintained, but I could always make them better. After I finished it was about two hours later. Nai was very satisfied with the style I had done with his locks. The cost for maintenance with a style was $50; however, Nai had given me $150. I asked him immediately asked him was he paying ahead of time for his next appointments. He told me that the other $100 was my tip and he would like to set up his next appointment as well as set up a time tonight when he could meet me for a date. I politely told him that I didn't date my clients. He then asked me could any of my employees could do as good of a job as me; because if they couldn't then he would have to keep asking until I said yes. It took Harrison pulling me in the office and almost laying me out for me to say yes.

The irony in it all was he still paid me at every appointment until this day. Everyone was none the wiser until of course after we got engaged.

"Oh, I almost forgot. I have something for you." Nai jumped up out of the bed like a child at Christmas. "Open it." Nai handed the small silver metallic bag, with a blue and silver ribbon to me; Blue was my favorite color.

"Nai, what is this for?" As I pulled open the ribbon and pulled out a small silver box. When I opened the box my eyes immediately started watering and tears fell down my cheeks. Underneath the box inside the bog was a white handkerchief with a lily on it outlined with blue just for me, Nai had thought of everything. "Oh, I love you so much, baby." Tears kept falling. In the box was a 2 carat princess cut pale blue diamond solitaire. Nai wiped my tears with the handkerchief and removed the wedding set from my left hand.

"You are my rare diamond and now you have the physical proof. Clarice will you do me the honor of continuing to be my wife?" Nai had started out on his knees, but ended up placing me on his lap as he placed the solitaire on my left ring finger. "Baby, I love you forever. I have meant those words before I found the courage to say them to you. I fully intend to say and mean it even after there is not a

single breath in my body."

"Mr. Harley," I had stopped crying, "You are just too

much for me. You are completely amazing. I know I don't

deserve all of this. When I think you can't love me enough

or that I don't need anymore reasons to love you, you show

me more." I wanted to say more but my emotions started

taking over. I was overwhelmed with so much love and

appreciation for Nai. I was happy.

The silence that I felt between us was more than any

words could mean spoken. Nai pulled me close to him. He

began kissing me gently on me lips, slowly guiding my lips

apart allowing his tongue to explore my mouth. The passion

of our love at that very moment caused my body to fall limp.

Succumbing to his every touch and command. Nai began

touching and squeezing my firm round bottom shapely thighs

as continued feasting on my mouth. He then began moving

downward to my neck, pausing at my spot, I let him know I

was his for the taking. I let out a purr that sound made

his manhood grow even harder and the veins in it pulsate;

yearning to feel my warmth. My nipples grew instantly hard

as he insatiably licked sucked and gently nibbled on each

one. He is always, taking his time to make sure of my

satisfaction. Nai licked a slow moving trail with his long

thick tongue around the curves of my breasts and down to my navel. I love it when he teases me as he travels to my sacred center. Nai had a serious method to feasting upon 'his wife'. Before he would even go near my clitoris he had me climaxing. I have no idea how that man does it. He would begin by licking the lines along my hips, making a trail from one hip to the other. Since I always shaved it made it very easy to continue his trail from the center of my bikini line to my outer labia. He stroked them so carefully and slowly. He would then use his tongue to open them up and stroke my clitoris. He would take long hard strokes from my clitoris to the opening of my hollow. Nai loved the smell and the taste of my juices. He slowly moved his tongue in and out of me embracing every moan and quiver that came from me. Each time that I climaxed he drank my juices in as if he had an unquenchable thirst. When he finally could no longer bare not feeling my inner muscles tighten around him, he rose to face me. Nai then, placed a gentle kiss on my lips. He lifted my body toward him and let me down slowly with every inch that entered my hollow. He never had to ask the reassuring question that all men ask, 'Whose is this?' Nai knew the answer so asking the question would be a moot point. Although every man know that has a good woman knows that if he messes up, she could

be gone before he could blink. Hence the reasoning for Nai
consistently telling me that he cherishes my being his wife.

"How do you want it tonight?" That is the one question
he always asks. From the first time that Nai made love to
me, he gave into to the fact that I was much kept and that
I had my moments where he would say "the real Clarice"
would come out. They were just moments. I always deemed it
strange for me to just let the whole world know that Nai
was sexing my brains out. I always held the concept in my
mind that a woman that has a good thing, (good dick or good
sex) from a man; should never let her secret out unless she
is willing to share. I've always been one selfish female
when it came to my man. Sex or no sex, the moment some
other female stepped to him she could have him that is if
he let her do it. Most of the time that was the case for me,
I was the safety net until my man decided he wanted to live
dangerously so to speak. Nai was the first man to accept
all of me; to not only love me but stay loving me. He was
the first man to embrace my shy nature in our relationship.
Helping me to become uninhibited when it came to him,
realizing that I like to be controlled in the bedroom yet
still have control. Now I definitely became more
uninhibited in our marriage. Nai even made me write it in

my vows. He reminded me that we were entering a marriage, a partnership which required that we both make decisions as he put it firmly, 'I am **not** taking on a silent partner'.

"Just the way you are giving it to me." That was my reply as I grabbed onto his shoulders. Nai knew what I wanted just by my physical reaction. Nai thrusted hard and slow while pulling back just far enough so that the head of his manhood was still inside of me. I love to be submissive so you know what my favorite position is…Doggy style. We went on for what seemed like days; what was actually hours. I think we even created some new positions in the process. That man sure gave me a work out, but my baby can say the same thing. My husband is the most passionate man I ever met. I ended up falling asleep in my lover's, my boyfriend's, my partner's, my man's, my husband's arms. Nai is and will always be everything to me. Nai hadn't bothered to wake me, he was used to me sleeping on him, and he almost preferred it. Little did I know while I was sleeping he was plotting for the surprise he had in mind for me in the morning.

Revisiting the Past

Seven years ago.

Nai pulled into the driveway and opened the garage door. Parking the car and closing the door back with the remote. He wondered whose car was that parked in front of his door. He shrugged it off thinking it may have been one of Dana's girlfriends. She was off today so it was no big deal.

Nai was coming home to tell her the good news. Nai's loan was approved; he had bought the building, at a cheap price. He had stopped by the jeweler; because today was the day he was planning to propose. Nai loved Dana. Although his mother warned him about her, even she had grown to accept her. But Nai knew better than that he knew he mother only tolerated it as long a he was happy. Little did he know the big change that he was expecting today was not what he would be what he had in mind.

As he entered the kitchen and locked the door, he called out to Dana.

"Dana, are you upstairs? I have some good news."

No answer but he did hear music. She always played music while she was home alone.

"I'll just go upstairs. She'll be happy to see me anyway."

As Nai reached the top of the stairs, he started to here more than just music. Dana was always changing things around, but this sound was different. At that moment Nai was hearing more than thuds or bumps. This was a clear bang, and then he heard a sound that was all too familiar to him. That sound was the loud moan of his woman when she comes to a climax. That could be what he heard. Maybe it was a porn tape she was watching. Maybe it was the neighbor. Nai was in denial because he knew the moment he opened the door to their bedroom reality would knock him down flat.

Nai stood in the doorway. More than anger, hurt, or sadness he was in disbelief. This wasn't happening. Instead of crying out because of happiness with Nai on his knees asking her hand in marriage; Dana was crying out for another reason. She was on her hands and knees telling some nigga named Eric, 'harder, I love it. Keep going, don't stop'. Words similar to the ones she had spoken to Nai 5:00 a.m. this morning. Hear he was 12 hours later listening to her telling this man the same thing. In their bed, in his bed in their house, his house going at it like it's nothing. He waited, in shock.

Surprise and Assurance

When I woke up Nai was looking down at me with a big
grin on his face. "Why are you looking at me like that?
What time is it? What did you do? I know you did
something." By now I was sitting up. Nai just continued to
smile as he picked me up out of the bed.

"Will you stop asking a million and one questions?
Girl, chill out and let me do this thing." Nai carried me
into the bathroom; the tub was filled with a hot milk bath.
He even used my favorite Victoria's Secret scent
Strawberries and Cream.

"Okay, you are trying to take my mind off of things,
you fixing a bath for me is pretty much normal. What did
you do, Nai?"

Placing me down, and removing my night gown, which I do not recall putting on. "Just get in the tub girl damn. Wasn't one of the vows you took not to question me?"

"Me, question not at all, supportive and submissive yes." I said as I got into the tub, beckoning my husband to join me as he always did.

"Well how about you practice that submissive thing."

"I believe I did that very well last night, don't you think?"

"Yes but right now it wouldn't hurt either. Come on baby you are supposed to trust your husband."

"Oh I trust you, but that is not the point. You only smile like that when you are being sneaky. Now tell me Adonai David Lavi Harley, what did you do? I started to get out of the tub. Nai knew I meant business when I said his whole name."

"If I agree to tell you will you get back in the tub?"

"Yes."

"Then I agree. Now let me assist you in proceeding to take a relaxing bath." Nai helped me back into the tub and cradled me in his arms. He then started soaping me up and starting with my back, moving to my breasts, my stomach. "First I called L.C. and asked him if he could handle the paperwork at the shop. He said he could and that it was just payroll, invoices and bills. What he couldn't understand was why you were planning on coming in on our anniversary. Of course that was well after you fell asleep and I washed you and put you in your night gown. He asked if I would come by the shop and check to make sure everything was cool. Amaris had to go to school early so that worked out perfectly. I stopped at the market before I came home. I fixed you a fruit salad just the way you like it, watched you sleep while I ran the bath water."

Experience taught me to control my temper. By now I realized that it had to be at least 11 am. The fact that Nai was now massaging my neck and shoulders calmed me. "I can't even get mad it you this time. What time is it?

"It is now 11:45 am, you were up late."

"Nai, why did you let me sleep so late? I had to do more than just sleep."

"Clarice, you more than got your workout last night. Look at your body baby it's beautiful. I don't understand why you stress over it so much. You showed me what you looked like before you lost the weight. Baby I still would have fallen in love with you regardless."

"Nai just like you always say you have to make sure I don't go any where, I have to be sure of the same thing."

"Baby girl, I know your morning routine like that
fourth line on your left pinky finger. It's why when we got
this house I had a small pantry and refrigerator added to
our bedroom. I know you are not a real morning person, so I
did all that so you would have whatever you needed at your
finger tips before your work out. Baby you need to learn to
relax and chill out. One day is not going to cause you to
become instantly out of shape. Some times I swear all you
see when you look in the mirror is everything that you have
risen above. First of all you haven't been the size you
used to be in what six years? You are not at single parent
anymore you have me to keep that burden off your shoulders.
You have an excellent support system in your family and
friends. What else can I say to convince you that you have
it altogether except for one thing, and that is to sit back
and enjoy life? Be proud of the person you have become for
once without digging into the past or thinking you can do
one more thing better. Be satisfied with your life.

I couldn't help but listen to Nai intently. His
voice always seemed to affect me so that I was hypnotized.
He was right, most of the time he was always right when it
came to my insecurities. I also know why Nai gave me my
ring last night instead of this morning. True he had played
my emotions to his advantage in more ways than one. But if

my hubby wanted to spend the day with me or at least most
of it who am I to say no? He had thrown me off my schedule
a little but thanks to my husband's interference my plans
for our anniversary were set into motion. My baby was smart,
but I am much sneakier. "I know baby I just worked so hard
at everything, even keeping your attention."

"Here we go. When will you learn or listen for that
matter? The day that I met I had already decided I wasn't
going anywhere."

Nai couldn't help to be frustrated with me. Here it
was our 5th wedding anniversary and I was feeding into my
own low self esteem. I just don't know how to rid my self
of something I've had most of my life. This is a milestone
anniversary for us especially in this day and time. I was
always about average size at least between 20 - 30 pounds
over my ideal weight once I hit puberty which unfortunately
for me was all too early, I was 11. I was active as a child
cross country, track and field, cheerleading, ballet,
volleyball, soccer. All the activity stopped when I got to
college. With that and my choice in birth control I had set
myself on a course of a downhill battle with my weight, or
should I say uphill. My lack of self esteem aided in my
becoming an emotional eater. You know the drill if I was
sad I ate, angry I ate some more, my boyfriend cheated on

me I ate, I stepped on the scale and saw how much I weighed I ate. The one thing that did keep me from gaining that freshman 20 twenty was I worked so much and well my child. I needed to be able to keep up with her. I had my limit. I would also diet on and off constantly so although I may not have gained weight and may have lost a few gained the few back I stayed about the same. When I reached my pitfall was the summer I was unemployed and I went on at least 25 different job interviews. I can truly say I had become depressed but the time I got a job I was barely fitting in my clothes and I got on the scale I weighed 275 pounds, had a double chin, my stomach could not be tucked in, I actually had cellulite in my thighs, oh no this had to stop.

I had started once again on a diet. This time it would be a change in diet more water, smaller meals, I dust off them exercise tapes. By that time I was 22, nearly two years later I was 268 and actually happily, with someone. But that didn't last long. This man was the straw that broke the camel's back. Kenneth oh I loathe that man. This man got out of a relationship that wasted 4 years of his life and made me jump through every hoop just to get close to him. When we finally got close or so I thought this selfish Negro decides that he wants to have himself an epiphany. Oh great! One of those, the excuse of all excuses. He being in a relationship or marriage wasn't for him, just because some gold-digger cheated on him. I had started my process of revamping me, Clarice Taylor Trueheart into a new person. I was taking drastic measures I went for a consultation for gastric bypass surgery, I had lost self control and needed to get it back. I had the surgery two months later. With the drastic change in my diet and vigorous exercise regimen the weight just fell off. I had declared that but the time my 26th birthday rolled around I was going to have the total package, pretty face, smarts and a body to make men and women's jaws drop alike even if I never found someone to share my life with. In that year's time I had lost the weight, got my cosmetologist license, was engaged to Nai and was preparing to go to medical school; which I finished everything early and started my Pharmaceutical company. I did all that and yet my simple ass can not bask in all my blessings. I still see that fat chick struggling with her daughter trying to go to school. I need help.

"Clarice Taylor Harley, baby I love you. I wouldn't care if you did go back to that weight, with the exception of me worrying about your health. I am not leaving, do you get that, do you understand that? I love you now, and a little extra on you will not budge me, might even make me hold you closer." By now my dimples were showing I was feeling a little better. Nai took me by the hand and lead me over to the long mirror to look at my biggest critic, me. As usual I always try to hide my body which even at a size 6 was hard to do because I was still naked. Nai pulled my arms to my sides. "Why do you still do that? Look at them abs, look at that booty turn around, girl. Look at it I'm waiting for some extra something to come on that so I can see it jiggle. You are 135 pounds I can lift you up with no problem. Check out the curves, full breasts, curvy hips, round tight booty, long toned legs. You honestly think that you are slipping?"

"Well, I did have that cheese cake and a steak."

"Oh my God, girl why are you looking down? Them soft pretty lips, pretty teeth, pretty smile, long dark lashes, mesmerizing maple brown eyes, help me out here. What is it that you don't see? I promise you baby everyone woman I was dating I called the night you said yes to go out with me on our first date I was done. The bad part is, I never told you this but, I had a date that night and I cancelled it telling her I had a woman and I was dating her starting tonight. I still would have done what I did if you would have said no. That night my mind, my heart, and my soul said you were the one."

When I looked in the mirror my biggest critic was gone it was just me and Nai. The smile that was on his face said it all. "Nai I love you so much. You are absolutely right. I apologize deeply honey it is our 5th wedding anniversary and her I am being selfish. You are such a good husband."

"Baby there is no need to apologize. I am here to fulfill your needs as you are here to do the same thing for me. But baby you say to me all the time that I make you so happy, yet we are still dealing with the issues you've had in the past. What are you holding on to baby, please tell me. What is it you are afraid of?"

"Okay you know what let's just move on from this. Baby I am fine. From this very second we are continuing to enjoy our anniversary. I didn't give you the present I got for you yet." I pulled a black box from under the bed with a white bow. "Here you go hubby." I had a smirk on my face that just barely showed my dimples.

Nai opened the box, inside was a black lace teddy with a pair of matching lace panties, garter and a matching shoes. Nai smiled slightly as he lifted the lingerie from the box and placed it on the bed. In the bottom of the box was an envelope with his name Adonai. It read:

Mr. Harley,

You know there is much more in store. Look behind your closet door.

Love,

Clarice

Nai opened the closet door and there was a custom made tuxedo hanging there. A one of a kind JB original design. My daddy was a tailor so you can guess how easy this gift came to me, and the fact I knew my husband's measurements so well. I wasn't the only so called sleeping dead in this house. Sticking out of the breast pocket was a nice size list of things for Nai to do. Like I said Nai was good but I was much sneakier. I kept in mind that Nai had to pick up the matching wedding band for my ring, which I am not supposed know about. I told you I was sneaky, but you will see later. He would have just enough time to get back to the house to get a shower and change for our "dinner reservations", the renewing of our wedding vows.

As soon as Nai stepped out of the front door, I called L.C. on the walkie - talkie. "Where are you now?"

"Whoa, what's up sleeping beauty? Prince charming left the castle yet?

"Yeah he just balled with my 'Things to Do' list. So check this out I have to pick up my parents and sister from the airport in 45 minutes."

"Right."

"I need you to pick up Sheree from the train station in an hour. Amaris gets out of school in a half an hour so you have plenty of time to do both. Nai already knows she is getting a ride from school so that is straight."

"Okay I hear you boss lady." We both laughed.

"My father has my dress so that was easy"

"So reminded me why is it again that you needed a new wedding gown?"

"Because Harrison, I was heavier when Nai and I got married. We are renewing our vows, emphasis on the 'new'."

"Okay I got you."

"Now I need you to go to the airport and pick up Tamia after you drop Amaris and Sheree up. By the time you get back everything so be in order and going according to plan for the ceremony. So all you have to do is get ready for the ceremony and make sure the arriving guests are seated."

"Will do Ms. Trueheart."

"Bye."

I headed out the door. I picked up my parents and sister, then made a quick stop to the jewelry store to pick my blue diamond earrings my husband bought me and my groom's new engraved wedding band. Then I drove straight

home so everything could be finished in time for the
ceremony.

***

    I tried on the wedding dress once more so Daddy could
see if any final adjustments had to be made. Of course
there weren't any my father is the best.

    "Daddy you are the best of the best. This is perfect I
only came to Baltimore once the whole time."

    Justin Barrett Trueheart, my father was the reason why
I was always soothed by a man with a deep voice. That was
my daddy, an average height man of five feet eleven inches;
slim build with curly salt and pepper hair and beard on his
dark brown complexion. The light brown almond eyes, soft
full lips and white teeth and smile were a perfect
complement to his appearance. The eyes, lips, teeth and
smile were something I got from him I don't know where the
gray line around the color of my eyes came from but that
probably came from my mother's family. I my grand father
had brown and green colored eyes, I think they might have
had gray in them however none of the children he and my
grandmother had inherited that from him. It seems I'm his
only grandchild with 'pretty eyes' or descendent for that
matter.

When I saw my daddy smiling, I knew exactly at that
moment what Nai was talking about. "Baby girl you look
gorgeous just as or even more so than you did five years
ago."

"Thank you daddy. I have got to get out of this dress
now so I can get ready. Plus Harrison will be here so with
Tamia so that I can get my hair done."

"Okay I am going to head down stairs to help your
mother, Trish, Amaris, and Sheree in the kitchen and get
things set up out back."

The front door beeped as L.C. and Tamia came in. He
always had a key to every place I lived in, I always
trusted him to that extent, as was the same for him. Tamia
began to work her magic so my hair would be lying just
right as always. As the hours went by the guests started
arriving. Each guest was given instructions to be ready to
be picked up by escort to attend the ceremony, including
his parents. No clues were to be given. Only a dinner
setting for two would be left. The reservations were
already cancelled as of yesterday, but course my hubby
didn't know that little bit of information.

Moving Forward

Nai arrived home at 5:15 pm. He put everything away and noticed candle light in the dining room and the smell of his favorite dishes in the air. "But she couldn't have cooked, we have reservations at 7:00 this evening." Nai thought to himself. "Baby! You home, are you upstairs?" Nai saw a note on the bed next to a fairly small box.

Happy Anniversary Mister Harley. In the box is some new cologne that just says Adonai. Wear this along with your new tuxedo and be out back dress and ready by 6:05 p.m. I love you forever.

Nai did just as the note said and was ready at 6:00p.m. He always made a point to be early. "Our reservations were for 7:00p.m.," Nai thought aloud "so whatever she is planning is cool." He went down stairs and when he got to the patio door…

"Oh damn, she got me. Everyone is here. Hey Mr. Justin, how are you doing sir?" Nai reached to shake his hand. "What's going on?"

"Are you ready to marry my daughter?"

"But, uh Mr. Justin uh I am…" Nai looked down at his left hand no band. Nai hand taken it off this morning before bathing as he always did. "I got you now. That's my girl she is so smart. Yeah I am ready, nothing will change that."

The look on Nai's face when he saw me appear through the patio door was like fireworks on the Fourth of July, Memorial Day and New Year's Day at midnight all in one. I wore an off white evening gown with a short train, princess sleeves, and a hand painted floral design lace cover on the bust, soft curls with baby's breath in my hair. My smile set things off even better, there was a time in my life when I felt that I would never be married much less renewing my vows on any anniversary.

At precisely 6:45 that evening, once again we were pronounced Mr. and Mrs. Adonai David Lavi Harley.

***

The night was fulfilling and fun. I managed to successfully plan the evening just the way I wanted it. It was complete surprise to him right down to Nai's parents coming. The man actually had tears in his eyes, he didn't even cry when we got married everything was perfect.

"I can't believe you got me, crying in all that good great stuff. I love you so much. I mean you even had bishop calling you Clarice Taylor Trueheart again and that gown. How did you get it here and hide it from me? And the Justin Barrett original, baby you are good." Nai had a huge grin on his face now, like he had a surprise of his own waiting for me, something I couldn't change or cancel. *Hum what could that be?* I thought to myself.

"It was simple. The dress didn't get here until today and the tuxedo has been here for two weeks hidden in Amaris's room. You are used to me buying shoes all the time so that wasn't a problem. My matching necklace, earrings, and bracelet I picked up at jeweler's today, poor man he can resist my charm. I was still surprised he told me before I could even ask. They did set off the gown and my ring and you had already paid for them."

Nai lifted me off my feet and proceeded to carry me through the dining area, living room and up the stairs to our bedroom. I had one more surprise set in place. I had arranged to have the room set up down to having the door cracked so Nai would have to work so 'hard' to get it open.

"You are really showing off; Girl I swear God knew what He was doing when He made you. You out did yourself, almost." There went that big grin again.

"Why is that?"

"Because I managed to have something else set up for you. Close your eyes and follow me."

Nai didn't have to tell me to open my eyes. As soon as I heard my baby grand playing I wanted to know who it was. Nai had hired a pianist to play and sing for me.

"May I have this dance?"

Nai took me by the hand, and we dance around the room. I was in a dream world.

"I had this planned for when we came home from dinner but since you cancelled those plans I guess we are even."

"Oh, wow, baby look at the time. Oh my God baby, our guests. We've been up here for all this time. How could I have been so selfish?"

I started down the hallway to the stairs. Before I could get five feet Nai had my waist pulling me to him.

"Baby the only guest here is the pianist and he already made himself at home because he's downstairs now getting a plate. You didn't even notice that the music stopped. This is our closest family and friends they are fine. Nobody will be mad if I steal a few more moments alone with my wife. I haven't seen you all day and when I did see you, you were walking down the aisle to me. That was dirty how you had me running around on our anniversary. So the way I see it you owe me girl."

I started smiling hard, I knew he was right. "Yes my husband, you are right, I worry too much don't I?"

"Yes you do. It drives me crazy but I love you even more because of it. Let's go down stairs."

***

"Man I am still trippin' off the look on you man's face when he came through the patio door." L.C. said as he shaped up the facial hair on his client.

"You know I was still getting glamorous for my grand entrance, but the look when he saw me was momentous." I was doing my thing with my client as well.

"Yeah you had that man crying and all." L.C. laughed. "Only you could make that man's eyes weld up like that. I got to hand it to you he is whipped, but in a good way. The bad part is you didn't do anything, he was treating you like his wife from the beginning."

"Yes my man does love me…" I paused for a moment as I put the finishing touches on my 9:00 a.m. Saturday morning client and counting my pay on the sly as I always did. "…I believe at this point I can confidently say 'he ain't going any where'."

"Yeah man, you are right about that, he would be a jackass to leave you especially at this point. Nai definitely knows what he has unlike them other simple minded niggas you used to date, especially the last one, who made up his mind when you decided to leave."

"Who, Kenneth, not that I forgot about him but I do have what exemplifies completely a real man."

"True but you know I will always be waiting for the moment he messes up too." We both busted out laughing. "But seriously Kenneth was a total ass when it came to his feelings for you."

Kenneth Charles Williams was fine and for all the wrong reasons because his attitude was ugly. Somehow I managed to be attracted to him. Especially, when this man still in the back of his mind wanted his ex-girlfriend. I could never understand for the life of me why any man would chase after a real bitch I mean in every sense and

definition of the word acted more like the animal than
anything. This chick sucked him dry and tried to pull more
from him after that. She even managed to coax him to
continue to be friends after all the pain. 'Hold onto a man
even when you don't want him so he can't get what he
deserves a real woman.

As I said Kenneth was fine, he stood six feet four
inches tall. He had a medium build, green and honey brown
eyes, commanding deep voice, the kind that could scare you
if he shouted and milk chocolate brown skin. He had the
privilege of experiencing my hair care skills back in
Baltimore. Kenneth's one flaw was the ability to cease
closer. Yet I was the one being accused of not being able
to let go. And still his actions proved true to form, he
managed to maintain a friendship with every ex-girlfriend
he had. But me I have issues because I cut all ties with my
ex-boyfriends. Yet he never showed real emotion. My past
relationships always ended badly, they always had to cheat,
couldn't just leave they had to hurt me. Maybe I set myself
up, nah not a chance not every time, to always leave broken
hearted, no.

I was myself with him from beginning to end. My flaw I
wear my heart on my sleeve. No matter who I was with they
always knew how I felt. He had suckered himself in to a

dead relationship with his latest ex, four years big whoop, but I had to pay for that, dumb ass. Our argument would always be the same.

"You are ridiculous, Kenneth I can not believe I am still hear this bullshit. I am not her, I am better woman. I don't ask you to pay for a damn thing extra for me. You are still obsessed with her that is you problem, 'because it ain't me. That is why you can't commit to me, more like refuse. Just let it go she has already moved on to what she feels is a better prize so you do the same. Let her be a part of his life and not yours."

Then Kenneth plays dumb as usual. "Oh my God, girl what do you mean? I don't know what you are talking about. Lauren has nothing to do with our relationship."

"No even, all I hear from your lips is not 'Clarice let me get a kiss' or a hug for that matter. Hell, it would be nice to know that you are in this relationship too. I may not have a cute little shape but I look good and I am pretty. There are plenty of men that are attracted to me and will have me just the way I am with no problem. But for some reason I chose to be with you. Yet all I hear is 'I did this and that for four years' and you weren't married, damn. She isn't the same person you met then and she isn't going to be. We are in a relationship, when will you wake up?"

Things didn't change so I just did what do best take me out of the picture.

"Whoa, girl what are you doing?"

"I am moving out. Kenneth I can't be with a man who still after two years is in love with his ex-girlfriend and most importantly does not love me. Or at best does try and doesn't want to try."

"How didn't I try?

I just shook my head as I took my luggage out the door. "You just did, you never showed or told me you that you felt that way. You can't even bring yourself to say it now. So I see no reason to stay. Good Bye Kenneth." I walked away with my head hung low, tears in my eyes, depression set in full gear. He heard me crying and even then didn't come, he didn't care.

Even now as he walked though the door of my place of business I feel nothing for him but disgust. I refused to a part of his laundry list of ex-girlfriends he keeps as friends. I always believed that was just his insurance policy for an option or a way out. This jerk even had the nerve to have a huge grin on his face looking right at me. Not only that; everyone seemed to know who he was here for.

I move out of the state and yet he finds me here in Atlanta.

"Hey sexy, long time no see." He took off his sunglasses.

"Hi." I know he sees the look on my face.

"That's all I get from you? Damn, you must still hate me huh?"

"Kenneth, I really don't have time for this, as you can see I am running a business here."

"Well, how about I give you some business?"

"No thanks, Kenneth. Come with me to my office."

"Gladly."

***

"What do you want from me?"

"Well the truth is that I was in town on business. I
needed my hair done a so happened to run into this dude
that just got his hair done by you. He just told me where
the shop was. I wasn't going to let anyone else touch it."

"I guess I'll by that, because you couldn't have just
looked me up since I never told you I was moving down
here." I sat down at my desk with my head resting on my
left hand showing off my wedding set.

"Damn, girl you married!???"

"Are you surprised? Oh yeah because you didn't want me
that was it for me and I would never have anyone to love me
completely. You didn't things out when I left?"

"It is not that at all."

"You know, I never did thank you."

"For what, I am lost?"

"For being a real jerk to me; you the day that I left
was a chance for you to redeem yourself and you didn't. It
caused me to put my off switch on permanently. I managed to
rid myself of that crazy, emotional, unstable, insecurity
and most of all that stupid big heart I had. I adopted the

'bitch' mode you were so fond of. The funny thing was my curt attitude is what caught my husband attention, so thanks a bunch."

"Wow I really hurt you, huh? You know every female I have dated since you left never measured up."

"That's nice Kenneth. Look the past is just what it is, I am over it. I am happily married now, with the man I want who loves me unconditionally, I have the body I want, and the life I want. Now your head does look a mess, the price is $45. Now if you don't want to pay you go find some girl in the hood and let he mess it up."

"Oh no, it is worth the price whatever it is to have you do it."

"Good now hurry out of my office so I can do your hair because I have other clients that I see regularly and you will be infringing upon their time."

"Oh you didn't know I'm not just a walk-in I have an appointment."

"Let me just take a peek at my appointment book, nope No Kenneth here."

"That is because I had the girl put the initials G.E.M."

"And what might that stand for?"

"Green Eyed Monster, I did realize that I was the one who was jealous. That I gave you every reason to be insecure in our relationship. If it means anything to you at all, I apologize."

"Although it is a moot point, I will accept your apology. But at this point you are going to make me late for an engagement I have later."

"Oh what is that?

Kenneth was always nosey he just never admitted to it. He just preferred to accuse that other person of trying to be all up in 'his personal life' as he liked to call it. He had a habit of making me feel not apart of his life yet always had an opinion on my friendships and personal choices. It made it so hard to feel comfortable in my own skin. I had just celebrated my fifth wedding anniversary and here this jackass was rattling my chain again. Nai was my other engagement, I will so much better when he comes to get me. I rode in with L.C. "If you must know I have a date."

Kenneth was confused and I left it at that as I began shampooing his hair.

The X is Back

As I placed the finishing touches on Kenneth's hair
her date arrived right on time, it was 2:00 p.m. Nai was
looking sexy as usual. Truth be told he was actually early
he had an appointment with L.C., Nai wanted that barbershop
feel. From the chair to in front of his wife. Nai had on a
black leather jacket, red button down shirt, olive green
cargo pants and black Rockports. When Nai greeted me it was
obvious that Kenneth was turning two colors; green with
envy and red with embarrassment. Being the conceited
epitome of arrogance he just knew that he was better
looking than my husband. That thought quickly went away
when Nai walked up to me. I was more than happy to make the
introductions.

"Hey baby, you are right on time I was just finishing up. Nai this is an 'old' acquaintance of mine from Baltimore." I was beaming inside. Nai was finer and dressed better than Kenneth's quote 'fine ass'.

"Kenneth this is my husband Nai."

Nai new this was my ex-boyfriend I just used the acquaintance to piss Kenneth off. "Good to meet you man." Nai extended his hand and Kenneth took it. "Maybe if you are going to be in town for a while maybe you can come over for dinner." Harrison was about to bust out laughing but caught himself. "I am sure you can remember that wife can cook."

That invite was about boasting that I was I was <u>his</u> wife as well as being hospitable. As I said Nai knew all about Kenneth. He just wanted him to feel humiliated, it work to a tee.

"Maybe the next time, I'm about to head out of town in a few days."

Try a damn month he practically tried to give me his whole schedule while we were in the office, hoping to have some time alone with me. Kenneth just paid me for my services $60 even, he read the price list he didn't want to feel sheepish as well. He wished us well on our date.

Kenneth might have held his high when he came in here but, he left with his head low and his tail between his legs.

***

'Great minds think alike' as they say. My man and I always complement each other, but today we had it down to an exact science. Nothing was planned just listen. You already know what Nai had on right. Well it is the same color scheme. I had on my black hip length leather jacket, my off the shoulder shirt with a mix of olive green, red and black. I have a pair of olive green cargo parachute pants tied at mid-calf and pair black pointed toe 3 inch high heel shoes.

"Whoa, baby girl um. You look good. But um, what were you spying on me this morning? I thought you were sleep."

"I was certainly not up at the crack of dawn like you. Did you forget you were trying to get some morning loving? And to no avail might I add."

"You are right baby, you were too busy trying to sleep we are just that intoned to each other."

We were holding hands as we rode down the street and onto our date. Nai just had the Jeep washed and detailed I could tell. He always changed the mats in there when go that done. Fall was coming to an end but it still felt good outside. Nai turned on the heat on my seat anyway, I was always cold. There was nothing like warm soft leather to sit on, Auto-start was a wonderful thing.

"Baby how are you feeling?"

"Oh, I'm okay, just a little tired but nothing unusual." I tried to give him a genuine smile but I couldn't hide the fact that Kenneth being here bothered me.

"Don't you know I know you better than that, girl? Come on now, L.C. told me that Kenneth was in here a while before you even started his hair. So fess up, don't be holding things back you know better than that."

"Yes seeing Kenneth after six years did get to me. But baby I set him straight before he could even flirt. I let him know I was married, happily and I have moved on."

"Um Hum." That was all Nai could say to that. My man knew. I couldn't fool him for nothing. Besides at this point I couldn't look at him because all those old feelings had come rushing back. I felt fat again, unwanted, insecure and lonely all over again. In a few hours that arrogant nigga managed to bring all that out of me. Everything that I worked so hard to move past all those years ago.

"Nai, I'm for real I am okay really." By now he knew that I was on the brink of tears. He pulled over the truck, unbuckled my belt, moved his seat back farther and pulled me to him. His touch was so gentle even when he was firm. He ran his fingers through my hair which was halfway down my back; another thing I managed to fix when I left Kenneth. Thanks to my own creative genius I managed to nurse my hair back to health.

I can not believe that man can still push my buttons and make me cry. He I am sitting on my man's, my husband's lap and I'm in tears over him. I have got to get it together. The buck stops here. Nai and I are supposed to be enjoying each other. I love him so much.

"Clarice as long as I breathe, not another man will bring harm to you, I promise you that. I want you to stop crying though. You are beautiful, brilliant, an excellent mother and a damn good wife. His loss is surely my gain. You know hell could freeze over ten times and I am still not letting you go."

I had to laugh at that one, he was using one of my phrases. "I feel better now, baby. Where are we?"

"I scoped out this park some time ago. Let's get out the table is not far. Grab the blankets off the back seat. I'll get everything else. You already worked hard enough today."

This man had everything planned out. He had a spread for the table, and a blanket to sit on the bench. Nai had

bought all of my favorite foods. It felt like our first
date. I was still working on losing the last 35 pounds for
my goal then. I really hope he is not planning on me
playing tag with him - not in these heels.

"Baby, can you look in that bag for me and see if I
left my ring in the small inside pocket?" Oh no he didn't,
he had his wedding band on the other ring I see it. What
else does he have in here? "Oh and Clarice I packed a pair
of tennis shoes to match your outfit." Oh yes he did,
that's my man.

"And why is it that you feel I need these?"

"Because after we eat I have other plans for us; Oh
there is another shirt for you too. You can change that in
the truck?"

"Excuse me, you thought of everything huh, Nai?"

"Yes including when playtime is over." Nai always
thought everything out to the last detail, he always saw
the big picture and then put the detail in. I love that
most about him, because I am the same way.

"What happens then?"

"Ah, the element of surprise, I know you are just
dying to know."

"Oh come on Nai, don't do that to me. Just give me a
hint."

"Nope. You know I'm not doing that, so what do you even ask?"

"I was just hoping you would give me my way." By now I had my tennis shoes on. I stepped into the Jeep so that I could change me shirt. This man was amazing, nothing more needed to be said.

"Tag, you're it!" Nai was off, that man was fast but he wasn't running as he could. We were playing a game so you know he had to give me a fair chance." I think we ran after each other for an hour. He certainly gave me a work out. When we arrived home I could think of nothing but lay my weary behind down on my bed. I need to re-energize just to take a shower or better yet a good soak in the Jacuzzi.

"Woo, baby I need a nap or something, not to mention a bath. I not exactly smell like a flower. You gave me a serious work out."

"Oh girl please, you barely broke a sweat. Besides, I'm not done working on you yet." Nai picked me up and put me over his shoulder, then proceeded to carry me up the stairs to our bedroom. Man when I think of our bedroom it is the most beautiful ideas that is a reality to me. When I say that when I was in my mid-twenties I had hit a low on the self esteem scale I mean it. I don't even think that the most unattractive person in the world could have felt as unwanted as me. I had given up completely and that rendezvous with Kenneth brought it all back. There has got to be a way I can get rid of these demons, spirits, what ever you want to call them they got to go! I have a gorgeous man that is smart, business savvy, he owns his own business, his financial planning skills are genius, he is always well groomed, he is saved (thank you Jesus), and most of all he loves me with every fiber of his being and I know it. So why am I tripping, why do I think that he is going somewhere? By now Nai had let me down and started working on my neck. Girl, that man knows how to bring the attention towards him. I'll just nibble on his ear in the mean time.

"Baby I want you so bad right now. I can't take it. You taste so good, I wanted to ask you to stay home today but I didn't only because I had plans for us tonight." Nai was telling me all of this in between kissing on me. I could certainly tell that he really meant what he said because for the first time every this man ripped an article on clothing off of my body. What had gotten in to my husband I don't know. He couldn't have had all this sexual tension build up from just this morning. What is up with my man? I'm not wearing that shirt again that is for sure. Maybe… nah it could be jealousy, Nai has never acted on

jealousy before. But it could be that now he knows that my
ex-boyfriend still wants me. Wow, I never experience this
before. I'm glad it is winter because he is leaving passion
marks everywhere on my body.

"Nai, honey what's up?" I had to stop him for a moment
he was like a mad man in the truest sense of the phrase.
"What has gotten into you? We did just spend the whole
afternoon together."

"Baby, I apologize. I guess it's just a bit of
jealousy. I don't want to lose you, you mean too much to me.
I mean seeing how that nigga just looked at you in front of
me even just sent my blood boiling. He still must not have
that much respect for you. I love you so much baby I'm
serious. I hope that you never doubt that, because I mean
it with all of me, every inch."

"Nai you don't have to worry. You have me no other man
can take your place, in my heart, my mind, or at my side. I
love you forever that will never change."

Nai continued his war path on my body but to a much
gentler beat. He feasted on my breasts one at a time making
sure not to miss a single inch of them. He played with my
center as he did this. I grabbed on to his manhood and
stoked along with him. His touch always sends shivering
chill up my spine. He caressed my thighs as I raised them

slightly. Then he licked a trail in between my breasts, to my navel, along the lines of my toned abdomen and down to my center. He took pleasure in devouring my center and my juices as I came over and over again. Nai would always take his time with me. As result causing me to let go of my insecurities, at least for the moment. Of course I returned the favor of pleasuring my husband's manhood. I made a point to make sure that my husband would be the only man I gave this kind of pleasure to. I would keep going until he couldn't stand it and he had to enter me.

Nai knew what he was doing when it came to making love. When Nai touched me places I never knew would cause arousal did just that. He is a very sensuous man when it comes to pleasure. He always made sure I got everything I needed as well as what I wanted.

"Baby, tell me how you want it. Please don't be shy with me tonight. I need you to go there with me. I need to hear you, to feel you; I need that aggression from you that I know is inside you."

"Baby, you know I want nothing more than to please you..."

"But, what I know there is one."

"No there isn't one not tonight baby. I'm going to give you exactly what you need." I grabbed hold of Nai's head and pulled him into a deep passionate kiss. "Now what I need for you to do is lie down and let me do what I do."

"Yes, ma'am." Nai had a huge grin on his face.

I climbed on top of Nai and began grinding making sure he felt everything. I need to get my anger out. I was not angry with Nai of course, just angry at myself. I knew exactly what Nai needed. I saw the looks Kenneth was giving me and even now make me want to throw up, just at the possibility of any thoughts he might have had. Tonight I would show Nai that he never has to worry about me going anywhere. I tried to do every position with me on top I had ever read about and even some ones I didn't. All I know is that I did what I set out to do and please my man I did.

"Woo baby, girl you tried to wear me out. Where did you get all that from? I mean baby I truly believe we are ready for that shower now. Because I think if we sit in the tub we might be sleeping in the tub." We got in the shower and washed each other off as we usually do, oiled each other's bodies down and as usual I took the top half of the pajama set and he took the bottom. I used to read books this that scenario all the time. That was part of my fairy tale and now I'm living in it. I was curled up in a ball as I always did lying beside my husband.

"Um, Clarice you know if you stay like that I can't sleep. I am already raising baby."

"Oh sorry baby. Is this better?" I said turning to lie on my stomach with my left knee raised.

"Now you are teasing me."

"No, not at all. I am doing no such thing. I am just getting comfortable."

"But you know that is an excellent entry position."

"Ah, I see you are getting your energy back. Well, maybe in the morning mister, we have to get some sleep because it is now 1:30 in the morning and we have to go to church, I am not going to be late."

"As I always say it is not like we have to lie on the altar and pray for forgiveness of our sinful ways; we are married."

"Ha Ha, that is cute Adonai, now go to sleep. Good night, I love you forever my husband."

"Good Night Baby, I love you forever my wife."

Decisions

Why is that I believe that I don't have it together?
This is crazy I have the world practically at my finger
tips. Am I crazy? Was Kenneth right about me? Only one way
to find out, I have to ask an expert. I need to know if I
am just being insecure, that I just never embraced the
confident woman inside of me. To the business world I'm
savvy, confident, sexy, powerful, and above all brilliant.
To my child I've always been superwoman, loving, strong,
and reliable. To my husband of five wonderful years, I am
gorgeous, brilliant, sexy, loving, loyal, and the perfect
wife. The wife meaning I keep his well our house clean, I
provide the peaceful atmosphere he always desired as a boy
growing up. I keep him happy in all aspects of you lives. I
mean there was a time in my life; well you could just say I

didn't give a damn. That demon or spirit of loneliness is horrible. Don't get me wrong I keep myself up so to speak, my hair was decent, my clothes were clean not always hung up or folded neat but clean, I always smelled good, my breath wasn't bad, I just wasn't happy. I mean even now I can stand the sugar coated words, big boned, heavy set, 'curvy', voluptuous, solid, chubby, oh I could go on. You get my point. Even now as Nai is sleeping and I am looking at me in this bathroom mirror this live seems so unreal, starting with me. I never dreamed I would have a body like this, even now that feeling of fat is there, more so the feeling that I am not good enough. I am for some strange reason waiting for the other shoe to drop. I am waiting to come home and find some tramp in the bed with my man. I am waiting for the day Nai says to me 'you know baby I am just not feeling this anymore our marriage is over.' I was surprised that I wasn't signing annulment papers soon after we got married. I was sure that he was going to wake and realize I wasn't the woman for him or worse I wasn't the woman he thought he married. I just don't understand why I am feeling this way. Oh, you wouldn't believe it on top of all this anxiety I am pregnant. That test on the bathroom counter is flashing in big ass letters PREGNANT. My daughter is fifteen almost grown, pregnant? But Nai is

going to be so happy, oh I got so much going on right now,
These beauty supply stores and spas are about to open
starting next month, one every month for the next four
months. I hate throwing up. I hope he doesn't hear me. Now
I got to call the doctor, I am still calling the
psychologist. Oh, I always wanted more children though. Oh
my God why am I tripping? I got to call mommy and daddy.
Darice Bailey Trueheart is going to be elated another
grandbaby. And Mr. and Mrs. Harley their first grandchild.
Oh, let me take my time on this one it has been a minute
since I experienced this.

"Nai baby wake up, wake up." I whispered in his ear.

"Good morning." Nai looked at the clock it was 7:50
a.m. "Why are you up so early?"

"Baby I have something to tell you."

"What is it, what is going on? Did something happen?"

"Nai slow down." I started smiling, he was really
confused now. "Take a look at this." I handed him the test
still flashing PREGNANT. The look on my man's face was like
a baby's first smile and how timely since we are going to
have a baby.

"Oh My God, baby a baby, um we gonna have a baby? You
pregnant don't play with me baby, is this for real? You at

this very moment are pregnant with my first child? Please don't let this be a joke?"

"No Nai this is not a joke. I just finished dealing with my morning sickness a few minutes ago. I am having your first child."

"Woo! Baby you have made me the happiest man in the universe not the world the universe baby!" Right then ear drums just pounded and my head too. "Oh baby, I forgot you hear is probably very sensitive. Baby stay right there I don't want you to do a thing. I'll take care of everything I'm going to make you breakfast. You had your bath yet?"

"Slow down cowboy. You are moving way too fast. I am fine. I am not helpless, I can still do everything I've been doing including fixing breakfast and washing myself. I know you are excited but don't you think we need to talk about this first?"

"What is there to talk about? You are pregnant with my first child no doubt, with our second child."

"You were right with what you said at first. Yes you have been Amaris's father for all this time. This is your first child and I don't want to take away from that. But Nai there is so much going on and about to go on right now. It's not exactly perfect timing."

"Girl are you out of it? This is perfect timing. We are more than ready to have this child financially or otherwise. Besides God's timing is always perfect or did you forget that?"

"You're right, I have no idea what I was thinking."

"I guess not because for a second there I thought you were talking about killing my baby. I wasn't about to let that happen."

"Oh no baby, that never crossed my mind. I love you way to much for that. I am in love with the idea of having you baby. So you are going to be my 'baby's daddy'?"

"Yes Ma'am, I sure am, my 'baby's momma'."

"Nai, we got to call our parents."

"Oh yes, how about we call them on three way."

"I think that is a great idea, but let's tell Amaris that she is going to be a big sister." Just as I said that my baby girl comes to our bedroom door knocking.

"Mommy, daddy is everything okay? I heard him yelling, and a lot of moving around." Amaris had her right eyebrow lifted when she was unsure of something as I always did.

"Yes baby everything is fine. Daddy is just really happy, really early in the morning. We do have something to share with you." I grabbed Amaris by the hand and sat her in between Nai and me. "Nai you tell her." Amaris had a slightly said look on her face.

"Amaris you are going to be a big sister. Your mother and I just found out this morning."

"Oh Daddy, wow I am so happy. I always wanted a little brother or sister. Mom how far along are you? Do you know what it is? This is so cool can I do your baby shower mommy can I please? You said I could do the next big event and I think this is big enough." We all hugged. This is one of the happiest moments in my life. Nothing I mean not a thing could take that from me.

"Amaris if it will make you happy you can do it baby. Shoot, I can wait to tell my mommy and daddy, another baby. Okay, let's call them so everyone can know." I looked at my stomach. "Now you know it is only because I love you I'm going to let you mess up my figure. Alright let's call the parents, well grandparents."

Big Announcement

We called Nai's parents first then asked them to hold on so we could call my parents, then we put everyone on speaker phone. I did the talking this time. "Mommy, daddy, Ms. Amelia, Mr. Isaiah Nai and I are having a baby so to you my parents ya'll are grandparents times two and to Mr. and Mrs. Harley congratulations on your first grandbaby."

Ms. Amelia spoke up first. "Amaris is my grandbaby too you know."

My mother spoke next. "Clarice, do you need mommy to come down there to help with anything?"

"Yes Ms. Amelia I am not taking that away from you at all. But as I told your son this morning it will be the first time you will experience everything from the beginning. I don't want this played down because ya'll think you will hurt my baby's feelings. Amaris who is right here with us is more than excited she even is going to plan the baby shower. Now where did she… oh never mind she is on the phone talking to her best friend about it."

"Okay baby, we were just thinking of our grandchild." Mr. Isaiah spoke up, Nai got his deep voice from him most definitely.

"Okay well I still have to cook breakfast and we all have to get ready so mommy and daddy I will talk to you later and…"

Nai interrupted me. "And mom and dad we will see you in church."

"Good Bye." They all said.

There is my phone, right on time Harrison.

"What's L.C.?"

"Not much just getting dressed you know."

"Guess what man I got something to tell you."

"What, what is it what's going? Do I need to drive over there now?"

"Boy if you don't calm down and listen."

"Okay, it's not bad right?"

"Nope."

"So what is it?"

"I'm going to have a baby."

"What?"

"I am going to have a baby. I am pregnant." I said slowly.

"Are you for real?"

"Yes I took a test this morning."

"Wow another godchild. That's what up. How does Nai feel about that? I know that man is so happy?"

Nai took my phone. "Ah, man I am beyond happy! I can't wait until her first appointment and get a sonogram to find out for sure when my kid is getting here."

"Okay, ya'll may talk about all that later. This is supposed to be all about me, thank you. I was telling my best friend about my pregnancy and I have to call the other one too."

"Oh sorry baby I am just so happy. You have to let announce it in church."

"L.C, I'm going to see you later." I turned to Nai. "Honey I know that you are happy about this. We need to wait until I go to the doctor's office and find out everything. I haven't even called the office yet. Baby it is only Sunday; I can't call the office until tomorrow."

"You are right baby I'm sorry I am getting ahead of myself. I just want to tell the whole world. I want everyone to know just how happy I am right now."

"Okay Nai right now you need to get in the shower so you can get dressed. It is now 8:45 a.m. We need to get moving because before we know it the time will have gotten away from us. I am going downstairs now to make sure Amaris is ready and make breakfast.

"Alright baby I'll see you down stairs in a few."

I head down stairs fully dressed. Normally I would just have my robe on over my undergarments but today with all the excitement time just flew by so I needed to get a jump on things. All I have left to do is my make up. I knocked on Amaris's door.

"Are you ready? I'm going to make breakfast do you want to help?" No Answer. "Amaris are you in there? I opened the door she wasn't in her room. "Amaris, girl where are you!!"

Amaris came running up the stairs. "Mommy I was cooking breakfast, well at least I started. You are going to need me to help out a lot more now that you are pregnant. Let's go downstairs and you can tell me what to do."

"Okay honey. Did you turn down the flame when you left the kitchen?"

"Yes, mommy that's the first thing you taught me."

"Good girl now let me see what you got going on here." Amaris had made eggs to everyone's liking, cooked bacon and smoked sausage, toast and started trying to make fresh lemonade. "You are onto a good start baby doll."

"Thanks Mommy, anything I can do to help."

"Do me a favor and tell your dad that breakfast is ready. By the time that is done I'll have some fruit cut up and the table set."

Amaris went up stairs. When she got to the top floor she knocked on the master bedroom door.

"Daddy are you dressed?"

"Almost baby, but you can come in." Nai was fixing his tie and grabbing his jacket it to put on. Nai's suit was chocolate brown, the shirt was olive green with a white collar, the tie was a mixture of shades of green and brown, the cufflinks were silver with jade colored jewels in them.

"Wow Daddy you look great."

"Thank you and you look just a beautiful as your mother. So what's up?" Nai starts to put on his jacket.

"Oh, well mommy says that breakfast is ready."

"Okay I am coming right behind you."

They came down to the kitchen Nai right behind Amaris. Look at my happy family and summer time next year this baby will have added to our joy.

"Wow look at you look exquisite as usual." I give Nai a kiss on his lips. "Our daughter really did it this time and I only helped with breakfast."

"Is that right you were down here cooking up a storm and I missed it." Nai had this big grin on his face. He looked so proud of Amaris.

"Yes I wanted to help mommy." My child is so sweet. I hope I can eat this. I'll start with the toast just to coat my stomach. I don't want her to think it was her if I throw up.

"Thank you, Amaris you have definitely help me this morning."

"Let's bless the food so we can eat, you know I'm starving." Nai always had a huge appetite.

I managed to make it through breakfast with all things that passed through my lips and to my stomach not to decide to go back from whence they came. Even the ride to church was free of morning sickness. We got to church on time and service was wonderful. Nai's parents of course fussed all over me, yet managed to keep it discreet so that not a soul would know that I was carry a child until we were ready for everyone to know. I must say I love that about his parents especially his mother because I know this was he doing. They insisted that we go out to eat. Amazing enough my

stomach was fine through dinner. We arrived home and I felt
really dizzy.

"Clarice are you okay? What's wrong, what going on? Do
you need to go to the hospital?"

"Nai baby it is just a side effect of being pregnant.
I'm probably a good way along. I just need to go upstairs
and lay down. I need to get out of these shoes, these
clothes have a cold drink of water which is upstairs, and
to lay down. I am fine baby."

"Mommy are you sure?"

"To the both of you stop worrying so much. I just need
exactly what I said."

Nai just picked me up and proceeded to carry me
upstairs. "Well the least I can to is carry you up stairs
and give you what you need."

"Nai sex ain't happening right now."

"No, I didn't mean sex though it would be nice but I
was talking about putting you into something comfortable
and getting you a bottle of cold water."

"Oh okay."

Just then my phone rang. Nai picked it up and began
walking out of the room. "Baby I'll be right back; I'll
take this it's probably someone trying to make an
appointment."

"Okay that is fine." He left the room and closed the door.

"Hello."

"Hello, Clarice you there?" A man's voice was on the other end.

"Who is this?"

"I was looking to speak to Clarice is she there?"

Nai started frowning. "This is her husband. What can I do for you? Are you trying to make an appointment?"

"Oh no man I just need to talk to Clarice. You can just put her on the phone."

"Look man you are not in any position to be making requests of that manner concerning my wife."

"I don't see why there is a problem with me asking for her since you did give me an invite for dinner some time."

"Check this out Kenneth, my wife really doesn't want to deal with you. My invitation was my being nice nothing more. I would think you know how to take things at face value."

"Okay you don't have to talk in code man. I know you saw me checking out Clarice. Who wouldn't for that manner? She is sexy as she wants to be. Yeah and when I met her she was still losing wait and trying to rid herself of your damage. Why don't you find another one of you ex-girlfriends to bother because this one has a man; Better yet a HUSBAND."

"Man please you are just a carbon copy of her ideal, me. You are just a slightly bulked up light skinned version with a different eye color."

"Get this straight I am a one of a kind original. There is not a thing about me like you. I know my place in my woman's life and that is to protect her, just like now. If she didn't tell you we are exactly newly weds, this marriage she and I are in has been on going for five great years. She is for the first time experiencing a man that really loves her and is not holding on to her for his own selfish reasons. Clarice loves me but you know that already don't you?"

"You are just holding my space man. She was just getting her practice in for her real man. Physically she left but mentally she still belongs to me. You saw her reaction, if you never should up she would gone to dinner with me."

"She told me about your proposal. That is how I know what I know she turned you down flat. Let me guess you picked up one of her cards and decided that you would call her today after she calmed down and would try asking her again. Well the answer is and will always be no. Why don't you save yourself the embarrassment and go back to Baltimore and be with one of your options. Let go of the fact that you can't have my wife and move on because she has. You can start by finding another stylist."

Nai hung up the phone without giving Kenneth a chance to answer. Just for extra measure he deleted the number and turned the phone off. He knew that she didn't leave the house number on her voice mail, which was unlisted anyway, but he would clear out any message Kenneth left her before she knew they were there. He then walked back into the room.

By the time Nai came back I was getting up to get a pair of sweat pants and a big tee shirt (one of his).

"Whoa what you doing, lay down. I told you I got this."

"Nai don't be silly. I am not helpless. I can get my own clothes."

"Yeah and my tee shirt on the top shelf, girl sit down."

"Okay, Daddy." I had a smirk on my face. It was just enough to change my husband's mood. I knew when he came in the room he had not set an appointment with a client for me but had just finished arguing with someone. I'm glad it was him and not me. I wonder if it was Kenneth it wouldn't surprise me if he had picked up one of my business cards.

Those two words made my man's whole shine. That huge white grin shined like the sun.

"Oh I can't wait until I hear those words from that baby in your belly. Now come here and let 'Daddy' hug you and take care of you. Hand over that bra and panties so we can get in the shower."

"Anything just to feel me up."

"You are right about that baby."

"I know that I am."

"I'm just trying to get it in when I can. Who knows when you may decide you don't want me touching you."

"Nai I wasn't like that when I was pregnant with Amaris. I didn't have anyone to touch me. I'm too affectionate for that."

"Okay I'm going to hold you to that when the baby really starts growing."

"You have my word."

The way that I felt as we massaged and washed each other's bodies was amazing. I felt the safest I've ever felt with Nai at that very moment.

"Nai I am so happy and honored to be your wife."

"The honor should be mine baby, you let me in at the most difficult time in your life. You share all of that with me, as if you knew me forever. You remember our first

date we talked until 8:00 a.m. and in that time you told me
nearly your whole life story. I don't know what you felt
with me then, it must have been safety. I wanted you to
feel safe with me then and continue to feel that way."

"Trust me I do. I don't need those sweat pants or tee
shirt. I just need you."

"You never sleep naked; not on purpose anyway."

"Well I feel like changing things up. I want to be
held tonight, skin to skin. I want your strong arms around
me to keep me safe and warm."

"I here that. MMM girl how about we keep each other
safe and warm. You feel so good I do not think I can go
back to what we were doing. If it gets too cold outside
we'll just have to pull out an extra blanket."

"I believe I have all the extra heat I need right here.
Kiss me man and stop playing you know you want me."

"Yes I do."

New Beginnings

    I love this time a year. It is almost Christmas and
New Year's is going to be wonderful too. I have an early
appointment with Dr. Anthony P. Raines my OB/GYN 8:00 a.m.
today. This is my second appointment and I find out the
results of my sonogram as well. I am now 11 weeks pregnant.
Nai has been fussing over me the past too weeks. He calls
me at the shop all the time. If I can't get to the phone he
is taking off work to see that I'm okay. I am just 11 weeks
now. The way he is you would think I was 11 months pregnant.
I love my man though. I am starting to get a little pudgier
around the mid-section now though. But to the rest of the
world I still look good for being nearly two and a half
months along. We arrived in the office; I signed in and had
a seat next to Nai.

"Baby this is it. We find out how far along you are officially. I wish we could find out what you are having but I know that will be coming soon."

"Yeah well as long as the baby is healthy I don't care."

"Mrs. Harley Dr. Raines will see you now." The nurse said.

"Can I come too?"

"Oh of course Mr. Harley you are always welcome at your wife's appointments."

Moments after we were seated in Dr. Raines office he came in.

"Ms. Clarice how are you? And hello to you too Mr. Nai."

"We are fine Dr. Raines. We were just discussing the sonogram."

"Great I have the results right here and pictures of your babies for you to home and share with all your family and friends. We were right about the due date well for one of them one is a day ahead of the other."

"What a minute whoa. Did you just say that I am pregnant with twins? Maybe I need to clean my ears out."

"Yes dear you are which is why you may be experiencing a small pouch around your lower abdomen at this point."

"How did that happen?" I looked over at Nai. He was just sitting there grinning at the pictures. I don't even think he heard what Dr. Raines just said.

"Well as you know Clarice sperm can live inside the vagina for up to 72 hours so your ovaries must have been working overtime lately and produced two eggs. One got fertilized one day and the next day the other."

"Look at the baby Clarice, look."

"Nai, honey that is not two sets of pictures of one baby they are of two babies. Whatever you did you did twice because I am 11 ½ weeks pregnant with twins."

Nai leaped out of his chair. "What! Twins, oh are you for real doc? I thought having one kids was great but two oh man. Wow Twins. Oh I am so happy."

"Yes sir there is two babies, fraternal twins, and two different eggs. So that means Madame you do need to take things easy. You can still exercise as I said before, but you are going to have to increase your intake of food and drink plenty of water and you may have to cut down on the number of clients you see in a day especially in about two months."

"I can do that, definitely. I am sure my husband will more than assist me with that task." I looked right at Nai with a smile. He smiled back at me and held my hand tight.

"You bet that I am going to be on the job. I'm keeping tabs on this hard-headed young lady every time I think about it. And now that I am going to be a father of two you know will." Nai was so serious.

"Well as long as Mrs. Harley adheres to my instructions, you won't have to keep as close of a watch Mr. Harley. How is your morning sickness coming?"

"It is more like all day sickness. I can barely eat a thing. I don't throw anything back up, but I stay so sick I don't feel like eating."

"Well I give you a list of things you can take over the counter. I would like it if you tried those first before I prescribe something for you."

Nai spoke up overly concerned as usual. "Doctor Raines what if she continues to lose weight? I have noticed some weight loss over the past few weeks."

"Well, Mr. Harley there is no need for concern at this moment. It has been a while since you wife has been pregnant. To add to it she is carrying twins which can be quite an adjustment for a woman. She will have to begin to try to eat more because in the next month if she doesn't I may have to put her on bed rest. Here is the list and a goodie bag so you can save some money. Infants are expensive no matter how well off you may be."

"Thank you Dr. Raines. Anymore questions for the doctor before we leave, Adonai? I thought not. I see you in a month and thank you again."

***

"'Anymore more questions before we leave, Adonai?' Really baby I was just trying to be helpful and supportive."

"I don't doubt that one bit, Nai. It's just that I am tired not to mention that little thing called morning sickness I got going on. I really would like to try some of these remedies to relieve this awful feeling I have day and night."

"Oh baby are you still sick? I'm sorry I thought you were feeling okay. I'm sorry. Well since I know you are off today then I'm not going in either."

"Nai you don't have to take off for me. I'll be fine baby, really. All I'm going to do is lie down and try to sleep this off. I know you have meetings today. Don't cancel them, trust me there are more days coming like this one."

"Well call me if you need me to come home. I mean it Clarice don't call no ambulance, call me. I want to know everything that is going on with my babies. That means you and the twins. Wow, twins man, how could I be more blessed than I am now? You gave me twins. I love you baby."

"I love you too." I gave Nai a quick kiss on the lips. I got out of the car and walked around to the driver's side of the Jeep and hugged and kissed Nai.

"I will bring those things you got on this list when I get home. Remember what I said don't play with me."

"Yes Nai. I understand perfectly, I will call you if I need anything."

The Unexpected

It was about 3 o'clock in the afternoon when my cell phone started ringing loud as day. But it wasn't someone I have in my contact list this was a new number. I knew that because I had just a plain ringer for that.

"Hello." I know I sounded sleepy as can be.

"Hey beautiful, what's up with you?"

"Who is this?" I knew it wasn't my husband or my daddy.

"Oh you don't recognize my voice."

"No I don't. Frankly whoever you are you woke my out of my sleep. I don't have time for games. So state who you are and what it is you want so I can go back to my nap. Otherwise clear my line."

"Damn Clarice. It's Kenneth I was just calling to see if you could fit me in today."

Oh my God this man is not still here in Atlanta. And calling me none the less, to make it worse he wants a damn

appointment. "Kenneth I'm off today. Why are you still here?
No I'm not making any house calls so don't ask because you
have you answer."

"Well I live here now. My job gave me the option to
stay so I took it. Besides I had to be near you what kind
of man would I be to you if I wasn't around. I am sure Nai
didn't give you the message that I called."

"Excuse me 'man to me'? What is that supposed to mean?
Kenneth you are not my man. I have one of those. I am very
happily married to him. In fact we are expecting twins we
just found out today. So I stand on solid ground that he
ain't going anywhere. So you can just pack your things and
roll right back up north to Baltimore Maryland. You are not
needed over here and haven't been need for a very long
time."

"Oh you can take care of that little problem. I'm sure
there are plenty of clinics around. If I leave you are
coming with me, you can take that to the bank. As I told
your 'man' the other night, he is just a place holder for
me. I'm back we can put the past to rest and pick up where
we left off."

"Where we left off was me leaving you after you
couldn't tell me that you loved me. That is where we left
off. As I recall our relationship, that you and I thing

wasn't happening. You had too many other distractions or at least one main one you could seem to get rid of by choice. I'm not going through this with you, Kenneth I don't want you in my life, please leave me alone."

"Come on girl I know you aren't happy. You can't be."

"Kenneth please get over yourself. I am very happy. I am happy with my life, my husband, my businesses and most of all with me."

"Just let me take you to lunch or how about you come to my place and we can talk."

"We have nothing farther to discuss."

"Just a couple of hours, Clarice."

"No, for the last time this is not happening. Leave me alone. I don't feel well and you are making it worse."

"Let me come to you and help you get well. What do you need from the store?"

"I don't need your help. Let me put it like this I am carrying my husbands first and second child. So this temporary position you think my husband has is more like permanent."

"Stop playing girl you ain't pregnant. At this point your daughter is almost grown. Why would you have a baby now?"

"Well believe it or not I am and nothing is going to change that. So stop harassing me and move on because I have."

"Then why are we talking?"

"Because you just want to here the sound of my voice. Kenneth, I am really not feeling well and you are giving me a headache. Please clear my line." I hung up the phone and turned off my ringer. Kenneth knew the deal it had been years but not long enough for him to know not to call me back. He knew it would be a waste of time.

What Next?

When I woke up it was three o'clock in the morning. My hunger bell was ringing hard. I have never been so hungry in my life. Oh I so do not want to get up right now. And what is worse I now really have to go to the bathroom. I did not miss this at all. I have to do this until July 4th. Okay I guess I have to start by opening my eyes.

"Nai, were you watching me sleep?" For the life of me I don't get it. Well now I know why I woke up, he is stroking my thigh. Okay I did lie down in a tee shirt, so why am I naked?

"Yes, I hope that wasn't a problem. When I came in you tee shirt was drenched. You were sweating really badly in your sleep, so I took the comforter off you and the tee shirt. I have to take care of my wife you know."

"Yes I know that. But you could have put something else on me."

"True but I love looking at your body and I wanted to
see my kids."

"You mean the pouch I have now?"

"My kids are in there, Clarice that isn't fat. I can
fully justify that because you are still exercising. Which
I think you should chill on that, but since the doctor says
it will help with labor later on and you have to slow down
at 20 weeks, then I won't complain much."

"I know but I still want to be sexy while I am
pregnant. I don't think that is possible."

"Girl, I am more attracted now because you are
carrying my kids and that won't change after you have
them."

"Okay baby, but if you excuse me I really have to go
to the bathroom."

"Oh, by all means go ahead."

I even feel myself waddling a little. I don't remember
this happening this early. Dr. Raines said it was because
of the twins. Am I done yet? One would think I drank ten
gallons of water today. Nai thinks he is so slick. He might
have been worried about me but he wanted some. He thinks I
didn't notice he was hard, please I know the precise moment
when his hormones reach his organ. There he is rapping at
the door I hope he doesn't come in I need solitude. Plus I

need a shower, bath something. Do I have any appointments today? Nope. I got to remember to tell Harrison that I won't be in the shop today. I'm sure Nai probably told him last night when he came in but just to touch bases. I guess I should answer him, did I lock the door? Shoot!!

"Baby why didn't you answer me? Are you okay?" I'm glad I was off the toilet. He looks so pitiful. "Well…why do you always have that blank stare?"

"Sorry I was deep in thought. I was trying to remember if I had any appointments today."

"No and even if you did they would be cancelled. I called L.C. too, he said he would handle everything."

"Thank you baby, but I'm going to call him a little later just to touch base anyway."

"Oh I took Amaris over there, L.C. said he would take her to school and pick her up so I can look after you today."

"Nai I am a big girl you don't have to take off of work every time I don't feel well. You will never get any work done."

"I can work from home. I'm making preparations for that now anyway. When you have to be on bed rest I'm staying home with you. We aren't discussing that. That is a done deal. I'll only have to go into the office maybe once a week for a few hours. Depending on how well you are doing I may take you with me."

"Okay Nai you are the boss. But I can always call you if something is wrong or I need to go to the hospital."

"Now you know that my office is too far away from home for that 'I'll call you if anything happens' especially the way you were feeling yesterday. I started to carry you to the hospital last night; I called the doctor and he said as long as you didn't have a fever its fine. He said it's just you body getting used to the extra blood."

"I know that Nai I am a doctor myself you know. My specialty is just different."

"Yes I know that. I felt like I was in school because I was up right along with you most nights. Let me run the water for your bath. You go lie down and I'll come get you when it's ready."

"Okay, I am still tired anyway." I think it wasn't longer than 30 seconds and I was out like a light. That ten minute nap felt like ten hours. Nai was picking me up off the bed.

"Come on baby, so you can get in this tub the water is just the way you like it."

"Thank you."

"I'll give you some alone time. I'll be right here in the bedroom if you need me."

"Okay. I'll keep that in mind." This feels so good. I love my man, he is just so right for me. I am so happy right now. My therapy is going well I am getting rid of all the past hurt and anxiety. Life is great. It only gets better from here.

* * *

After my bath I got dressed quietly and went down stairs to exercise. I am taking it easy despite what my husband thinks. I even invested in some pregnancy exercise videos. I'll just put this one in since I have a little more energy. I love working out with Davonda Allen. I read in a magazine that her two new after pregnancy videos will be out next week. I'm going to get them now so I'll have them after I push these babies out. She even has one that you can exercise with the baby or babies so I am certain to buy that one as well. Good things my hubby isn't having sympathy cravings. I'm hungry all the time when I'm not sick but my stomach is only the size of a golf ball, so I can only eat but so much at a time. Apparently the 'King' has risen form his morning nap. Good thing I started

cooking breakfast because he is calling my name like he is
ready to eat.

"Yes Nai I'm in the kitchen."

"I thought you were going to call me if you needed
something. I'm glad I smelled you cooking otherwise I would
have thought something happened to you."

"Yes but I didn't need anything. You were asleep and I
was enjoying my alone time. I know if you were watching me
sleep all that time you surely would be tired. I fixed
pancakes want some."

"Thank you. Can I have some kisses and hugs too? I
mean since you were sleeping when I came home."

"Oh yes." I love it when he asks for affection, not
that I don't give it to him anyway.

"Come here," He pulled me on his lap "I don't want you
to lift another finger today, you understand."

"Yes now can we eat before our breakfast gets cold?"

"Yes." He let out a deep belly laugh. "I'm starving
anyway."

"Really? Then how come you are all over my neck
instead on your plate?"

"You seem a bit more appetizing and I know you taste
good."

"Do I now?"

Are we there yet?

Five weeks and five days to go. It feels so good out
side I love the spring. I am humungous Nai keeps begging to
come to my sonogram appointments lately. He has been so
busy in the office lately he can't make it I have one every
week. He finally just said today he's going and he doesn't
care what is going on in the office. I told him his plan to
take off the last 8 weeks of my pregnancy wasn't going to
happen. Tax season is just ending for the most part and he
had so many audits to do. He did work from home some days
but he still had to go in for one reason or the other.

I know why he wants to come so bad, he wants to see if
I'm carrying two boys, two girls, or one of each. I know
the odds because the technician told me months ago they
were fraternal twins. Sheree wants to know too show she can
'start' my wish list for my baby shower. I went along with
it for three reasons: One Amaris asked me the day I found

out could she plan it, two I never had one with Amaris and
she is planning it with her godmother, three I need baby
stuff it's been a very long time. Nai and I bought all the
big things already. Just last week he made me buy another
truck. I do love it though. It's a 2007 Dodge Durango
Limited. You know how he got it straight from the
manufacturer that's my baby. It is hooked up just like my
Acura, but now I have customized navigation system with
satellite television and radio and a separate system to
play videos for the babies. Don't forget I do have a truck
already remember my Mary Kay Escalade, but my hubby says
that's for business. So I am giving my Acura to Amaris for
her birthday since she did get her license which all
happens today May 26.

        "Clarice come on lets go, if you take any longer we
are going to miss the appointment."

        "Okay Nai I am 34 weeks now I can't just run out the
door you know."

        "I'm sorry baby I am just so excited about seeing the
twins. Are you sure you are not going to back out this
time?"

        "Yes baby I promised didn't I? Besides I want to know
too I want to get some things when we leave the office
today. You know I hate returning stuff."

"Yes I know. Let me help you in. So is everything set the surprise for Amaris?"

"Yes dinner reservations are all set. I sent the car out for the works and L.C. is bringing it when he comes to dinner. She is going to love how her name is on everything. I am going to have the valet bring it around first when we leave."

***

"Good Morning Mr. & Mrs. Harley follow me please Dr. Raines will be in to see you in a moment." This was a different office; Dr. Raines would be doing the sonogram today. These babies are so active I feel like they are going to jump right out.

"Whoa ya'll got to stay in mommy a little longer okay. We are going to take your picture though."

"Yes we are."

"Hello Dr. Raines how are you?"

"I'm well. The question is how are you? Today we are going to use a different kind of machine. This one shows a great deal more detail. You will be able to see clearly all of the features."

"You mean I can see if my son looks like me. Oh man. Or and my daughter? Well you know."

Dr. Raines just laughed. "Yes Nai you will find out the sexes on the babies as well."

"Okay well can we get started? They are fighting for attention here."

"Okay well Clarice you can get up on the table and raise your shirt. You won't feel cold this time. This one also gives the heart beat at the same time."

"That's them??"

"Just a minute Nai, let it the doctor get it in position."

"Okay the one on the right side is a… girl. And on the left side… a boy."

"A boy and a girl. Baby you gave me a son and a daughter!! I thought I was the happiest man in the universe when you told me you were pregnant, I am truly that man now."

"Thank you Dr. Raines. You have made my husband a very happy man. He has been worrying about this for a month now. Maybe now we can move on to baby names."

Dr. Raines let out a heavy laugh. "You are welcome, the both of you. The twins are very healthy. Now how you got pregnant one day behind the other is amazing. The boy is older but as we saw your daughter is the boss of the two."

"Well we will see how bossy she is when she gets here." Nai said with a huge grin.

"We'll be going now, see you next week." I pushed Nai out of the day before he tried to convince Dr. Raines to induce me today.

***

"How was your appointment yesterday?" L.C. held the door open for me.

"Oh it went well. I have new pictures. Dr. Raines used a new type of sonogram equipment to look at the babies. You can see everything, look."

"Okay. I see now I have a godson and a goddaughter. I can't wait until they get here."

"Me either I am so tired of wobbling around everywhere. This pregnancy has been fun but I'm tired."

L.C. was laughing because as I was talking I was walking or wobbling over to my station. We had decided since in the other two salons we were facing each other that the master barber and stylist chairs would be side by side. They would also be in the center of everything. Well we were still opposite of each but our stations were connected. "I glad we did this shop the way that we did because if not I would have to run over to pick you up and other things."

"Yes well I wasn't planning on this pregnancy at the time. Just a different feel. I need to check my appointments for next month. The doctor said I am going to have to cut my days down working more. He said I may deliver next month so I think I may just be mentoring most of the time since we have those students coming from Empire Beauty School in a few weeks. I checked them out there are good. I love giving back you know."

"Yeah I know. I'm going to be in the office for a bit. I need to call my daddy and find out how Eula B Pearl E Pharmaceuticals is doing. Not that I don't already know but the new sun block reviews were supposed to come back yesterday."

"Sun block?"

"Yes. The product I told you I went up to Baltimore for to over see the production. I had to send the sample and the ingredients because we were so busy with the grand opening of Naturally Creative Beauty and Grooming Supply in all 5 locations, remember that two weeks we closed the shop and flew to Los Angeles, Manhattan, Philadelphia and Baltimore. The next week we did the party for the location

here in Atlanta. I want the sun block Naturally Screened to
be sold in the beauty supply chains we own."

"Ah did you for get you own that company solely?"

"Well, I don't I gave you 10% of the shares that means
you are an owner too. You are a stock holder. I want you to
be in Forbes magazine right along with me."

"Yeah but you bought those shares for me."

"Yes as a birthday gift. I am so excited everything I
started years ago is finally paying off. School, Mary Kay,
my pharmaceutical corporation, God is truly blessing me in
more ways than I can imagine. I would have never though
that I would be in Forbes Magazine much less on the cover!
I am a tycoon now. You hear me a tycoon. I am on top of
everything that is beauty and when I start my beauty
product line next year can't a thing bring me done but God
and I don't see that happening. And right by me will be my
husband, my kids, and my best friend and partner. Yeah I
Sheree and of course my parents, you know that."

"Yeah I am proud of you lady. You have really done it
for yourself. I always knew you would be big and you've
made it."

"Why thank you my kind friend. You truly showed more
confidence in me than I have in myself." We both laughed
but the statement was true. There was a time when I really

believed that I would not be successful at anything I
wanted.

"I am sure that isn't the case now."

"No it is not the case, I can confidently say that."

"I am glad to here that.

Low and behold when I thought that things were at
peace. Here comes that nigga, I haven't seen on heard from
him in months, since I found out I was pregnant with
McKenna and Josiah. He is going to send me into early labor.

Kenneth is persistent I will give him that. Okay Clarice,
just stay calm.

"Good Morning how can we be of service to you today
sir?" He looked good but his hair was a mess. I looks
almost like he hasn't had it done since I
told him I didn't want to be bothered anymore.

"Morning."

"My aren't we grumpy today."

"Look I need someone to take care of my head."

"And of course you came back to my shop for just that
purpose. I can not believe you."

"Can we talk in your office?"

"Sure, whatever."

In the office

"Look I know I told you to leave me alone."

"Clarice I'm desperate, I."

"Please stop, after the stunt you pulled. Talking trash to my husband, then calling me up and upsetting me. Well your little plan to stress me out enough to make me miscarry didn't work. As you can see I am still pregnant and will be having my babies in 2 months."

"Come on baby you know you don't have to stay with him just because you are pregnant."

"Kenneth, number one I am not your baby. Number two Nai and I will have been married 6 years in October. There is no entrapment going on."

"You know I'm the real deal."

"I thought that a long time ago. But I know now the real deal for me is my husband. Let it go you lost me for good when I left you almost 7 years ago. You are going to have to find someone else to be happy with, because it is not me. As far as your hair, business is business. I'll service you as long as you keep things on your end strictly professional. You know I don't need you for anything. I will be in Forbes Magazine as a new multi-millionaire. I am sure you saw my husband in it 2 years ago."

"Okay, I can't lose out on having you skills not being used on my head. Congrats on the cover too, I heard about it through a few connections. Can we be friends at least?"

"You lost that then as well. Strictly business." Oh I am so glad I will be off next month because I need all the rest I can get. Little did I know Harrison called Nai and told him what was going down. Of course Nai was not at work, well it was lunch time. But still I can handle myself. Let me get Kenneth out of my office before Nai flips out.

"Harrison, please take my husband outside of the shop."

"You know I can't do that." He was trying his best to be discreet especially since Nai was right in his face.

"Yes you can, tell him I want to take a walk and I will be out in a minute. Bye."

"Oh, are you trying to avoid a fight with your hubby."

"No, I'm trying to save you from an ass kicking. Now get out of my office and go sit at a shampoo bowl one of the girls will wash your hair while I am out."

"Whatever you say Clarice."
Of course I came out behind him. Harrison did manage to keep Nai up front. I swear I do not need my husband in Jail. Dr. Raines told me I really could go into labor at any time

after the first of June. I'm 32 weeks now, it feels like 302 weeks. Carrying two babies at once is no joke.

"Hi baby." I gave him a kiss and gently nudged him to go out of the door.

"What is going on? Why is Kenneth here? I was on my way back to work but L.C. called me. Are you okay? Or do I have to take my jacket, and necktie off?"

"Baby I have everything handled. I am fine. Kenneth is a client and I explained to him that as long as he respected the boundaries I have set he can remain one. Besides, after next month I won't be here for until the end of September and then it will be one a limited basis until the twins are 6 months old. Both of our parents will be here to help but I still want to be there and the little fact of me breast feeding is important."

"Yeah you're right. Don't make have to fight. I don't like it when you are upset."

"Nai I was calm the same as I am now. Just chill out, I told you I got this. 'We' are all fine. See that's Josiah kicking because he hears his Daddy. McKenna just turned over look."

"Hey son, hey Josiah you better not kick your mother too much or your sister." He is so funny he calms right down when ever the subject of the babies comes up.

"Nai can you get me a snowball? I'm thirsty and hot."

"Egg Custard and Ice Cream right?"

"Yes. I love you Nai."

"I love you forever baby."

Time is UP!

    "Oh my GOD!!! Ouch!!!." I do not miss this at all." I
am great full that I made it to 40 weeks but this hurts. I
don't remember all of this pain with
Amaris.

    "Baby what's wrong? Why are you screaming? Did your
water break? Do you need me to rub anything? Tell me what
you need."

    Every action causes a reaction. The pain wakes me out of
my sleep my scream wakes my husband. I'm glad Amaris is at
Harrison's house. Oh, I have to call my parents and Nai's
parents. Mommy and Daddy are going to be here this
afternoon. Ouch. Good thing Nai's parents are here. Maybe
one of them can go get my parents from the airport. The way
this pain is going McKenna and Josiah will be here in a few

hours. What time is it? It is 5:45 in the morning.

"I'm okay it is just a contraction. You can rub my back though, the pain is mostly there. But I need you to keep track of my contractions because they are coming. Ouch! Quickly."

"Alright just blow out. I'm going to rub your back. That was 5 minutes."

"Okay call Dr. Raines and let him know how far along my contractions are. His cell phone and pager is on the dresser. He's at the hospital already, he gave me his schedule."

"Okay. Hello Dr. Raines. Clarice is labor."

On the Phone

"Yes Nai. How are you doing?"

"Oh I'm fine but my wife is in a lot of pain."

"Well has her water broke? Does she have the urge to urinate?"

"No it hasn't. But I think she is getting up to go to the bathroom now."

"How far apart are the contractions?"

"They are 5 minutes apart."

"Nai, please help me to the bathroom."

"Nai are you there? Don't let her go to the bathroom."

"Yes."

"Okay, don't let her go to the bathroom get her overnight bag and whatever else she needs and bring her to the hospital."

"Okay."

"Call me back when you get to the lobby, so I can have someone come down and escort you to labor and delivery. It's a good thing Clarice pre-registered. Good Bye."

"Will do, Good bye."

"Nai I need you. Ouch!"

"Baby Dr. Raines says to take you to the hospital."

"Okay let me go to the bathroom first."

"No baby he said not to let you go to bathroom and to bring you straight to the hospital."

"Okay. My bag is in the bottom of my closet." I swear I have never seen Nai drive so fast. Thankfully he hasn't gotten a ticket yet. "Nai slow down baby you are going to get a ticket."

"No I am not."

"Yes. Ouch you are."

"No I am not. The reason is because I called my cousin Lance and he sent out a message to all units if they see my Jeep pass don't stop it. Also if they see my approaching, to put their lights on so that we can get to the hospital faster." No sooner than he said that an officer a head of us put his lights on to guide us the rest of the way to the hospital and one was behind us. It was a good thing to because I felt like I was going to push them out any minute. We arrived at the hospital and someone met us to take me up to labor and delivery. Amaris was at L.C.'s house so I'll call her later.

Two more hours of labor and McKenna Liana Harley came at 7:15 am 4lbs 1oz 21in and Josiah David Harley came at 7:30 am 4lbs 6 oz 21in. L.C. called and said that my parents called him saying they caught an earlier flight. So they will be at the hospital at about 10:30 am.

"Well my babies managed to come right on time July 4th." Nai was holding both of them. Of course McKenna was blinking her long lashes at her Daddy. This little girl had the nerve to have a hairdo coming out the womb. She was rocking a flip in the back of her head. Her hair was just that thick, so was Josiah's.

"Yes they are baby. They look so small in your arms Nai."

"Yeah Josiah has the nerve to be sleep after all that kicking he did. McKenna just gives me those long blinks you do when you are flirting."

"That is my daughter."

"They both have long lashes."

"Yes they do with light brown eyes with a star burst of gray in the middle. How did that happen?"

"I don't know maybe I'll ask my parents what my eyes looked like when I was born. It is amazing that their color showed up so early."

***

"Well good morning." No he didn't. No he is not here in my hospital room. Nai is going to have a fit the moment he sees Kenneth here.

"What are you doing here? How did you know what hospital I was?"

"Well your employees talk too much. We did have an appointment today. Did you forget my appointments were scheduled months in advance?"

"You didn't have to come you could have sent flowers."

"Your babies are beautiful. Have you reconsidered my request?"

"No and I am not going to."

"Come on Clarice what do I have to do to convince you?"

"Nothing, just leave. I'll see you when I get back from maternity leave. Good bye."

"Okay, think about it."

"Good bye, Kenneth." The nerve he makes me sick. I can't wait until my parents get here to see the twins. I think I'll walk down to the nursery to feed my babies I got a feeling they are hungry. I have to call and see if those special made nipples I designed came in. That will make things so much easier on everyone later.

I am so proud of myself. I am surprised that no one in all this time has thought of it. I had a cast made over my nipple and worked with the distributor that provides the materials that make life-like or like-skin products used in adult toys and constructed a nipple to go on their bottles. I hope Nai remembers to check when he gets my parents settled before they come. I want to try them out the next time I feed them. I am sure they won't know the difference.

"Hi Daddy. Hi Mommy."

My dad had this glow about him today. Maybe it was because I just gave birth to his first grandson. Amaris was his first grandchild. My sister Trish had decided not to have any children, frankly she never wanted any either. So, all the grandchildren would be coming from me.

"Where is that new grandson and granddaughter of mine?"

"Are they on their way or in the nursery?" Mommy was smiling too. I now surpassed my mother in the number of

children she has, my sister and I were her only two
successful pregnancies out of 7. Trish and I are 10 years
apart.

"They will be here in a few minutes. I am glad ya'll
are here because normal I have to get the nurse to bring
McKenna and then Josiah 20 minutes later, because Josiah
eats slower. Either that or the nurse will bring them both
and hold one for me while I am feeding the other. They've
been hungry every 90 minutes. Nai did you bring the breast
pump? Did the nipples come in?"

"Yeah baby they look so real. Did you ask them to make
them like this?"

"Well the ones for the twins anyway. At least for the
first few months I want to work on their visual growth and
their motor skills. So having the nipple of their bottles
look and feel exactly like my breasts is the ideal. Now
when I send the ones for sale to production I will give the
parents the option of ordering the real looking nipples.
Here are my babies let's find out if they now the
difference. Madison always eats with her eyes open so let's
find out."

"I'll put the milk in the bottle and feed Madison?" My
mother was more than happy to oblige. My father took Josiah.

I findings were correct they never knew the difference. I
think Josiah even sped up his eating.

What NOW!

    "David, there is a Dana Townsend to see you." What
Dana it can't be. I haven't seen Dana since I caught her
with her legs rapped around her ex-boyfriend's waist. I so
do not need this right now. She is so full of drama. What
does she want here, money? That was funny how I cut
everything off that day, cable, lights, house phone, cell
phone, and internet. She had to call me from a pay phone to
curse me out. I couldn't stop laughing. But hey what was
there to explain? I had seen everything I could even see
the sweat dripping off that man's balls. That is how much
in shock I was when I came home. I even went the mortgage
agent that sold me the house and told them to put my house
up for sale that day and I wanted it sold in two weeks. I
lease an apartment that day and moved in that night.

"Tell her to have a seat."

"Okay, David."

"Thanks Rachel."

I had all my clothes sent to the Goodwill and bought new ones. I started to have someone do the same to her clothes. I just had some movers to pack them all up and send them to her parents' house. Changed the locks and transferred the alarms system to my apartment. Called her job and told her all of her belongs were now at her parents house and she no longer had a home with me. All of our joint accounts were closed and any of her money which wasn't much was placed in a separate account. It's a good thing I hadn't proposed yet. My house was sold in three days. I had all my personal numbers changed and hadn't heard from Dana until now.

"Rachel you can send Ms. Townsend into my office."

"Well, Nai or should I say David, you have done quite well for yourself. Forbes magazine, GQ, Ebony, even seen your little wife on a few magazines and such."

"What is it that I can help you with Dana?"

"Well I was think that maybe you could give me a job. I mean you do know that I have excellent administrative skills."

"Dana I have an assistant, she is right outside the door if you would like a formal introduction."

"My aren't we testy this morning. I see you are still in love with me."

"Not hardly, Dana. I have been married nearly 6 years now. So since I can not help you with a position at my company, I can assume that we are done."

"Well I beg to differ. I wasn't looking for a position as your assistant but I did see that you have a need for a receptionist in you investment department."

"Yes Dana we are currently interviewing suitable applicants. However you are not one of them."

"Sorry to interrupt, David, but Clarice is here. She said she wanted to know if you were done with those figures yet."

"Not a problem at all Rachel. Please could you just send my wife in?"

"Dana I need to handle this it is business you know."

"I know that is your wife Nai. I saw you and her in Forbes a few months ago. But you must not be happy. I can see it."

"Dana, please stop it. Even if that were true I would never ever come back to you. Now I feel that we are done here so could you please leave my office? I may put a call into one of my colleagues for you, maybe they will have a use for a woman of your 'talents'."

Dana began rubbing Nai's shoulders. "I could just reacquaint you with them."

"Please leave, Dana." He moves her hands as the door opens.

"Hi baby, I…oh hello. My name is Clarice Harley and you are."

"Just leaving." Nai interrupted.

"Nai don't be so rude. Please to meet you." I extended my hand.

"Dana Townsend, nice to meet you as well. Thank you so much N- uh David. I supposed I be hearing from you soon."

"Yeah right." Nai mumbled under his breath.

"Who was that baby? A colleague of yours?"

"No that was the Dana."

"Really? Then why was she here, not to mention with her hands all over your shoulders?"

"I don't know, baby she claimed she wanted a job."

"Oh and what job would that be?"

"Baby please don't get upset. I did not know she even knew where my firm was. I had moved to this location a month after we started dating."

"I really find that hard to believe. Are you done with those figures. I need to get them to the bank so the New York salon location can get started."

"Whoa. What is up with the strictly attitude? Aren't we supposed to be having a late breakfast together this morning?"

"Here is your breakfast Mr. Harley, enjoy I have lost my appetite."

"Baby?" The door closes.

"Rachel it was good seeing you."

"Oh you too, Clarice. I saw the pictures of the twins, they are beautiful."

"Thank you."

***

I can not believe the nerve of that woman showing up like that. True Nai may not have known she was coming but I did not like what I saw. I guess it all begins now after the babies come the cheating. I'm back to my old size, no stretch marks or nothing. Can this really be happening? I know that is Nai. I don't feel like talking right now. Damn he's persistent.

"Yes, Adonai."

"Whoa. Are you mad at me? My name you said my name. What wrong baby?"

"Are you cheating on me?"

"NO!"

"Nai don't lie to me. If you are just tell me."

"Baby I'm the one scared of losing you. That I'm not good enough for you. Where is all this coming from?"

"Nai you can stop telling me that. I thought about I was a rebound for you. I remember you telling me that you had just broken up with her 3 months before you met me."

"Baby why does that matter? You were not a rebound. I was over her the day I found her having sex with another man in my house. We will be married 6 years in two weeks. Why are you having these doubts now? I love you more than ever now. You just had my son and my daughter, my first child, children. I love you."

"Nai, you don't have to say that if you don't mean it."

"Clarice I need you to stop tripping for real. I feelings for you have not changed. I don't care who comes in my office."

"I think we need some time apart. At least that way you can decide if you still want this marriage."

"I want you I want my family that is all I need. You want space from me?"

"I'm giving you space. Either me and the babies can go or you can. I think that is best."

"But baby…I"

"Just do it for me. I need this."

x = 2

"My favorite stylist."

"I Kenneth have a seat."

"Why you so sad? Hubby not doing his thing?"

"Kenneth don't cross that line or you can walk right back out the way you came."

"Aw, why don't you let daddy take care of you then you will be happy all the time."

"I am warning you, Kenneth. Leave my personal life alone."

"Okay, just know I am here for you."

"Whatever just go over to the shampoo bowl."

***

"David."

"Yes mom."

"There is someone here to see you."

"Who is it?"

"Boy just come on to the door."

"Okay, mom."

"Oh, I can not believe this shit!"

No this chick did not show up to my parents' house. I mean something has to be wrong with my eyes because I am not seeing this.

"What did you say Nai?"

"Nothing mom, thank you."

"This is not funny. You show up at my parents' house. What part of we are done don't you understand?"

"Well, I knew you were a little ticked at me showing up at you business unannounced."

"So you show up at my parents' house unannounced?"

"Well I wanted to apologize but, your assistant said that you haven't been to the office. Is everything okay at home?"

"Dana it is my business. The sign on the building does say Harley & Associates. Which means, I don't have to go in if I don't want to? I'm the boss I can do that."

"I know all that. You still didn't answer my question. Is wifey taking care of you?"

"Dana that is none of your business. I would really appreciate it if you would leave now."

"Okay I'll go. Here's my number if you need me. I'm always here for you."

"Yeah whatever get out Dana."

***

Well, well, well it seems Nai's assistant is away from her desk. Perfect. I just use these keys she left out to open the door. If I still remember I know Nai keeps a spare house key in his desk. Bingo. I'll just go 'home' and surprise my man. Clarice won't be there. She is too busy running her 'beauty' shop.

"Hmm nobody's home. Nice and spacious definitely bigger than the house we had. Well, when I get finished this house will be mine."

"Whose car is that in my driveway? It's raggedy and dirty. I know Nai isn't here. His mother called me this

morning asking when I was going to let him come home. I
doubt he is staying at his mother's house probably just
eating dinner there."

I sat my bags down. Good thing Amaris has the twins.
Nobody messed with the lock. Is that water running in my
kitchen? I don't like this. Oh know that winch is not in my
house trying to cook on my good all-clad cookware. Why is
she in my house?

"What in the hell are you doing in my house? I don't
even want to know how you got in here but you need to get
your ass out of my house."

"I'm here to reclaim what is mine. Obviously you
aren't taking care of home. Nai would be here otherwise.
What you used him to build up your chain of beauty shops
and make your first million."

"First of all I didn't even know his status when I met
him. Second of all Nai is my husband and I take good care
of him. Third if you would have read the article you would
know I earned every dime on my own and I started out in
Baltimore, Maryland not her in Atlanta, Georgia."

"Well, the fact still remains that Nai is not here.
And you are not making much of a home for him either. I saw
if today at his momma's house looking all pitiful. You a
trifling wife."

"Girl please. You are a stalker. I know he ain't been sleeping at his mother's house so try again. Why don't you just hand over my keys because I know you have them and leave my house."

"Please this about to be my house again."

"Again, this house was built from the ground up so what are you talking about?"

"Don't act like you don't know what I am talking about."

"No see this house here got my name on the deed. So he can't do me like he did you. Besides I know how to keep my legs open only for my husband. Oops that's right you mess up so you never did become his wife. I am the first the last and the only Mrs. Adonai David Lavi Harley."

"Whatever take as seat." Oh no she did not just touch me. Well I now have the right two times over to whip her ass. Here I go. One good hard punch to the mouth.

"Now see didn't learn not to run your mouth it will always get you in trouble."

"Whatever b-" Another hit right to the mouth. I just kept throwing punches I didn't care where.

"Whoa, Whoa. Baby get up."

"No, she shouldn't have been in my house."

"I know but baby her lip is busted and you got blood on you. Just get up please."

"Alright but if there is blood on my carpet. I'm going to continue what I was doing."

"There is no blood on the carpet. I will clean it up if there is."

"Oh my lip…you b-"

"Say another word and I'll swell up your eye."

"I'm gonna sue you."

"You can't you are trespassing. And in the United States that gives me the right to do what ever I will to you. You are a danger to myself and my family. So go ahead and embarrass yourself and try to sue me. Any sensible lawyer will laugh right at you."

"Dana I don't know how you got in my house but for real you need to leave."

"I ain't going nowhere."

"Oh yes you are. First you stole Nai's keys then you been stalking him. Then you trespass on my property. Can you say jail time. Oh not to mention you put your hands on me first."

"Dana just leave. It is only because I am holding my wife she is not going off on you, just go."

"Fine but this ain't over."

"Wait, put some ice on your big mouth." I did have some compassion. I did rock her jaw good.

"Thanks I guess. This ain't over. Nai you are going to see that you belong with me."

"Go Dana."

"You should have just let me whip her ass."

"Clarice you already did enough damage."

"Why did you care about her?"

"I don't it's just…"

"Just what Nai? That you been sleeping with her? She have you some, put it on you? So now you have to save her?"

"No, baby, look I've sleeping away from my wife and children for nearly two weeks now. I want to come home. I have only wanted you, even if it was just to hold you. There is nothing going on between Dana and I. I was pissed off when she showed up at my parents' house."

"I need to think and you need to leave. Go sleep where ever you were sleeping, I'll call you."

"Oh my God, she has our phone number too?"

"Clarice it's my office calling actually that's Rachel."

"Hello."

On the Phone

"Hi Clarice, how are you?"

"Fine."

"Listen is David around? I was concerned because his office door was open when I came back from the printers. He hasn't been in the office for a while so I wanted to know if he was there. I just need to ask if he wanted the locks changed to the suite if he hasn't been here. Nothing is missing though."

"Oh well hold on."

"Okay I'll give you a break about the keys. Rachel said your office door was open and she knows you keep it locked when you aren't there."

"Well I haven't been to work all week."

"And why not?"

"Because I've been in our getaway condo sulking over you."

"Really?" I wanted to believe him.

"Yes, look just tell…well give me the phone I'll tell her."

"Hey Rachel, thanks for calling. Listen call the locksmith and have them set a schedule to change all the locks on the inside of the building. Have them start with my office today."

"They said they can be up in an hour. Is that okay?"

"You are on the money, thanks. Yeah call them back and have them come now. I'll be there in about an hour and a half to pick up the copies for my suite. Just set up a schedule and email it to me. I'll inform everyone else myself."

"Okay, I'll get right on it. Good bye."

"Good bye."

"Where are the twins?"

"With Amaris thank God."

"Oh okay. Look I miss you. I just want to come home."

"Nai that woman came in our home because of you. I'm glad at least I hope she doesn't know about the twins. She could have hurt them."

"She doesn't know. Baby come on let me come home and we can talk about everything you want."

"I don't think so. And I'm changing the locks to everything else, my shop, the cars, and the house. You can decide it you want your truck locks changed."

"Clarice, I still trust you about the situation with Kenneth."

"Yes well Kenneth doesn't have the keys to our house and he hasn't shown up out of nowhere either. Kenneth please just give me a day."

That day turned into a week.

When a plan comes Together

"Momma I don't know how much longer I can take this."

"Well Nai you know what you have to do."

"But I've been trying for a week. She won't take my calls."

"Try again today."

"I just don't understand how one woman, just one could turn my world upside down like this."

"Life happens like that sometimes baby. It is just God's way of making sure you appreciate the good things.

Sometimes he lets things happen so your relationship with him will be that much stronger."

"But I haven't been taking anything for granted."

"Baby I know that. But because we are His chosen people things may seem more difficult for us than for others."

"I haven't seen my babies either."

"Nai I have a feeling things are gonna work out today."

"I hope you are right momma."

"I know I am. Just call her today."

***

"So how are things in married folks world."

"Kenneth I'm not for it today."

"I'm only making small talk Clarice."

"Sure you are. You know the drill so, get going."

"Yes ma'am. But you know I can make you happy."

"Kenneth I know that I said I was not for this today."

"Alright I'll be quiet. For now."

"How about period."

I am so glad I am finished this man's hair. I am about to go call Nai. I want my husband home. It's been two weeks. What was I thinking? I know that woman was just trying to see how happy we were and I just played right into her plan. I probably pushed Nai right to her.

"Wonderful job as always, here you go and here is a little extra special something."

I opened the card. It was a travelers' check card for $10,000. I can not believe he is trying to by me back.

"Kenneth you know you can't buy my love."

"I'm not trying to because I know I still have it. Can't you see you don't need him? You need me, you need us."

"Kenneth I have a family. And my husband and I have two new beautiful babies. I am not break up our home for you or anyone."

"Well your home isn't that happy, now is it?"

"All married couples go through a rough patch."

"Yeah but come on now have you even talked to him in the past three weeks?"

"We've talked."

"Another argument."

"We are going to be just fine."

"If you say so."

"I know so, and things are going to get better starting right now, today."

"Where are you going?"

"Don't worry about." I go to my office to call Nai.

Hmm, she left her cell phone out here. It's ringing. Let's just check the caller ID to see who's calling. The Husband, I'll just answer this. No need for her to speak to him. I'm just going to make double sure.

"Hello Nai."

"Hello. What are you doing answering my wife's phone?"

"Same reason you are calling her. Now let me tell you something. Let me just school you real quick. Cla-"

"Sorry Kenneth but that is my wife calling me on the other line. Let me guess you just got your head taken care of at the shop. Get off the phone."

"Hey baby I was just calling you."

"Oh you were?"

"Yes I've been calling you all week."

"I miss you too."

"I love you forever, baby. Let's make up. I'm sorry all of this got out of hand."

"No baby, I should have trusted you from the beginning. I let my insecurities take over. I should have never stopped therapy."

"Therapy? When were you going to therapy? How and why were you hiding that from me?"

"Nai I just wanted to work out my issues on my own. I made all of my appointments during the day. I wasn't trying to hide anything from you. I just thought that I wouldn't burden you with my issues anymore."

"Baby your issues are my issues. That could have helped me help you. I would have allowed me to see why you go in the bathroom in the middle of the night sometimes and cry. Baby we need that communication."

"Your right. I am sorry for that, baby. Would you come home and we can talk about everything over dinner. Amaris is going to be at your parent's house for the evening so it will be just me, you, McKenna and Josiah."

"That's fine for dinner but for desert, I'm gonna need all the kids at my parents house. I know how you are with them. I am not going for being neglected tonight. I got some time to make up for."

"Okay honey, whatever you want it is yours."

"Okay well I'll see you in an hour."

"Until then I love you Nai."

"I love you forever, my wife."

***

"Mom, you were so right. Clarice and I are going have dinner tonight to make things up."

"See I told you. Now just have Amaris bring the twins with when she comes."

"Well Clarice said it would be alright for them to have dinner with us since I haven't seen them in a while."

"I agree. But bring them over after dinner I miss them. I love spending time with all my grandchildren and your father too. You know he has just been in prayer since this whole thing started with you too. I'm glad Clarice got to that woman before I did. I had no idea she was the cause of all this until I heard your reaction. Then I knew something was up. How long had it been since you've seen Dana?"

"Not long enough. I'll bring them over when we finish dinner. I have to get my things from the condo anyway."

"You need to let that wait until tomorrow."

"I want everything back the way it was today."

"Okay. I'll see you later baby."

"Bye mom."

***

"So how did the call go?"

"Well. I am so happy L.C., I miss my husband."

"I know for a fact that he missed you. Ya'll can't ever fight again. I need my sleep."

"I'm sorry." I couldn't help but laugh. My best friend was caught in the middle. Harrison is such a good friend.

"It's alright. I'm always here for you. You know that."

"Yeah I know. Well everything is straight in here so we can go. I called Amaris and told her I was on my way but Daddy might beat me there."

"Yeah! You been holding out on the man for almost a month you know what coming to you." Harrison was smiling hard.

"True but he don't know what I got for him."

"Awe man. So um I'm just gonna plan to be handling things here for the next few days."

"Nah, I can't leave you hanging like that. I got clients."

"True but Amaris passed the board test so you know she can handle your clients. I watched her work while you were on maternity leave."

"Yeah my baby girl did her thing on some of my best clients. Oh trust the called me. But I told her exactly what to do, so she was obedient."

"Well let's get out of here. You need to get home and so do. I got a dinner guest. Oh thanks for the curry chicken recipe. This one is of Jamaican decent and I'm trying to see how well she likes everything."

"Boy when you gonna settle down?"

"When I stop loving cash."

"Okay let's go. I am not going there tonight."

Epilogue

You can breathe now

"Baby dinner was lovely."

"You liked that baby?"

"Oh yes the lamb was tender the veggies were just right. I'm ready for desert now."

"Oh well I made cheesecake with raspberry preserve, so after the dishes are washed you can have some."

"Oh you doing me like that."

"Yep sure am. Now get to washing."

"We got a dishwasher."

"Either way you are going to have to make sure they are washed so get to getting."

"Yes ma'am."

That man has never washed dishes so fast. He must really want some desert or some sex.

"All done."

"Let me see. They are all sparkling. Good job baby. Now here is your desert."

"Oh thank you. Oops let me get that."

"No see you did that on purpose. Go sit down and eat your cheesecake."

"Is that the door?"

"Yes it is I called Dad and asked him to come get the twins. That is one less stop I have to make. I still need to get my clothes from the condo. I really want it to feel like I am at home for good."

"Okay I'll go with you."

"No baby I'll only be an hour if that. I will call you when I get there and I'll call again when I am leaving."

"Okay make sure you call."

"I promise. It will be no longer than an hour."

"Give me a kiss before you go." He gave me the most passion felt kiss I ever felt. It sent a chill down my spine and right to my hollow. Only my husband could do that to me. I want him so bad right now. It is not so much in a sexual way. I miss his touch alone, the security that I need in my life. I miss him already and he hasn't even left yet.

"Baby I got to go now or I'm going to have to make love to you right on this floor."

"Okay, hurry back."

"I'll be right back."

***

I really missed being home. I want things to go back to the way they were. I really wish Dana hadn't brought all this drama to my life. Don't she think she did enough before our relationship ended. I can not believe it, Clarice was seeing a psychologist all this time and didn't tell me. I just hope that now she really understands that I am here for any and everything she needs. I miss my children. I can't wait until tomorrow. After church we are going to have a family day out. I want to have a picnic or something.

Wow was I speeding. It took me no time to get here.
Well let me call my Clarice and let her know that I am here.

"Hey baby, I'm here."

"Hey okay."

"I'm going to grab this stuff and then I'm out."

"Okay…I talk to you when you leave. I have something
special for you."

"Oh you do? What is it?"

"Can't tell you. You just have to wait."

"Okay, well I'll see you when I get back.

"Okay, bye."

***

"Baby, I'm home. Clarice? Where you at baby?" I left a
note on the counter for him.

"Okay, a note let's see."

Nai,

I am waiting for you upstairs. I missed you so much. I
never want to be apart from you again. I promise from this
moment on I will tell you everything. I promise that my
past issues will no longer be a problem for our marriage. I
thank you for being a wonderful father to Amaris and loving
her as your own and for being such an amazing father to
McKenna and Josiah. Come on upstairs to your wife.

Welcome Home,

Clarice

Nai just came up stairs and pulled me into a passionate kiss. I body felt limp but full of life and heat at the same time. I have never loved a person like this. Our souls are joined completely. Nai although he was hard as a rock and I know that he missed me was still gentle. He took such care as he removed my night gown. His touch is so full of warmth and love. He kissed every inch of my body. As he entered my hollow everything became right with the world.

"I love you forever, Clarice."

"I love you forever, Nai."

The relief had come and so did we. We were once again as ONE. Oh, you wouldn't believe it.

It is a wonderful thing to be me you see

Because no one can be me but me

Some have tried to imitate and duplicate the perfection

that is my being

Not professing my being as perfect but,

I am the best of what is my best

Of doing that, which is being me.

-Morgan Klarysse

Thank you for reading this tale. I hope you enjoyed it as much as I did. I am sure you will look out for the next tale.

Morgan

Morgan Robertson resides in Baltimore Maryland. She is currently a student at Towson University. She is single mother. Morgan has been writing since she was 13 years old including short stories, articles, and poetry.

www.ingramcontent.com/pod-product-compliance
Lightning Source LLC
Chambersburg PA
CBHW030251270626
47156CB00021B/1640